"Listen, Nan Gilliam,"
he said as he reached for her.

"I believe we have a long-standing score to settle."

"I . . . I don't have the slightest idea what you mean."

"The devil you don't! Nan Gilliam—" He spat out the words. "I didn't think I'd ever forget that name. You're the only person on earth who has dared threaten me."

Suddenly, he laughed, then lowered his face to hers and kissed her warm and full on the mouth. There was no hatred this time, only a burning excitement that began to build between them as he explored her mouth, probing, tasting, until she felt her bones begin to liquefy . . .

Second Chance at Love

EMERALD BAY
WINTER AMES

A JOVE BOOK

First Jove edition published August 1981

First printing

Jove books are published by Jove Publications, Inc.,
200 Madison Avenue, New York, N.Y. 10016

Chapter One

As she opened the door to the Pinnacle Realty office, Nan Gilliam felt the excitement begin to build as it had each day since she had first begun working as a real estate agent. She loved it. It was a job she could get her teeth into and momentarily forget things she'd rather not think about.

Taking a brush from her purse, she ran it quickly through her mass of hair which gleamed like burnished copper as it fell in a soft pageboy onto her shoulders. She smoothed the green sharkskin skirt over her trim hips as she decided that, if nothing else, the past few months had been good for her figure. She had lost four pounds right where it counted most.

Predictably, the phone started ringing even before she reached her desk. Laura, her boss, was on another line in her private office. She covered the mouthpiece and waved as Nan slung the strap of her shoulder bag over the coat tree.

"Your line's ringing, Nan. Sorry I can't get it. I'm talking to a client."

Nan sat down at the desk and swiveled around to face the telephone. Intuition told her it was Lance. She knew it just as surely as if she could see him sitting, feet up on the table, his blond hair combed in that precisely casual way down over one eye. Taking a deep breath, she steeled herself to refuse whatever he asked. She had done far more than her share. Now it was time to cut all ties with her ex-husband. Her voice reflected her determination.

"Pinnacle Realty. Nan Gilliam speaking."

There was a momentary pause, then a man's voice, obviously amused, laughed into her ear. "Look, if this is a bad time I can call back in ten minutes...the only thing is I'm calling from Los Angeles."

Nan let out her breath. "I'm very sorry. I-I was expecting someone else. Is there something I can do for you?"

"That's much better, Miss Gilliam. I thought for a minute everything had frozen over up at Tahoe. I'm Craig Martindale, producer, director...you name it, for Regal Studios in Hollywood. To make a long story short, I'm looking for a rental up at Lake Tahoe."

Nan pulled a pad of paper toward her and grabbed a pen. "Yes, Mr. Martindale. Will you be needing an apartment, a condominium, or a house? And do you have a particular location in mind? South Lake Tahoe, Tahoe City?"

He laughed. "Not exactly. I'm looking for a shooting location, a ski lodge overlooking the lake. A big place with an extra-large living room, country kitchen, a big staircase leading to the second floor. In other words, the works."

Her pen stopped in midair. "You plan to shoot a movie there?"

She could feel his grin over the telephone. "Right the first time, little lady."

"I...I suppose you know the cost will be outrageous," she said, cautiously feeling her way. It occurred to her, as she warmed to the subject, that the commission would also be outrageous.

"How long do you need the place, Mr. Martindale?"

"Don't know yet, but at least a month. We have to finish before the snow starts. As far as expense is concerned, the budget can handle anything within reason. The important part is that the setting is right as well as the interior. We'll need a large main room with the fireplace as the focal point . . . a big stone one, preferably. The furniture should be authentic antique—not Early American, though."

"Um. . . . How soon will you need it?"

"Yesterday."

"I hope you're not serious."

"Oh, but I am. We had planned to shoot it on the lot, but the backers opted for more authenticity—so we need a place as soon as possible."

"I've no doubt we can find exactly what you're looking for, if you give us enough time to . . ."

"Time, honey, is what we don't have. I know all the arguments so don't waste them on me. By the way, you might like to know that you came highly recommended. Foster Landon, head of Media Enterprises out there in Tahoe, said that you were the most energetic newcomer in the real estate business and if anyone could find me a place, you could." He paused just long enough to let the flattery sink in. When he continued, his voice was low and very persuasive. "Now are you going to do it for me or do I look elsewhere?"

Nan chewed her lower lip as she hesitated for a bare second. "Of course I'll do it. Can you give me a week?"

"Make it four days and you've got a deal."

"All right. Four days it is . . . but I think you should know, Mr. Martindale, that I'll have to move heaven and earth."

He laughed. "So what's the big deal? We do that every day in the movie business."

She joined in his laughter. "May I have your telephone number? I'd like to get back to you later this afternoon when I've had a chance to do some preliminary work."

"You've got it." He gave her the details with the fine precision of a computer, then, obviously convinced she would have no trouble fulfilling his every demand, hung up.

Nan leaned back in her chair and blew out her cheeks. "Great day in the morning!" She laughed at having used one of her mother's favorite expressions. "What a way to start the day."

Laura stuck her head in the door. "Was that Lance again? Sorry I couldn't . . ." She looked carefully at Nan. "Well, that was a stupid question. I can tell the answer by the happy look on your face."

The enormity of the assignment suddenly hit Nan and she sobered. "Dear heaven. What have I gotten myself into?"

"Knowing you, it could be just about anything. What's up?"

"Oh nothing." Nan waved slim, tapered fingers in a casual gesture. "All I have to do is find a mountain ski lodge complete with stone fireplace, a winding staircase, antique furnishings, a country kitchen, and oh yes, a view of the lake."

Laura snorted. "Which side?"

"Don't laugh. I'm serious. My client is looking for a rental for a month or longer, and money's no object."

"I hope he owns an oil well. He'll need it if you can even find such a place."

"Not an oil well, a movie studio."

Laura sat up quickly. "No kidding?"

"Well . . . he doesn't actually own the studio. He's the producer or director or something, and he's looking for a shooting location. His name is Craig Martindale."

Laura blinked a couple of times and her eyes took on a glassy look. "Craig Martindale?"

Nan nodded. "Yes. He got my name from Foster Landon who was a client of my father's law firm. Oh, that's right. I had forgotten that you used to be in the movies. Have you ever heard of Mr. Martindale?"

Laura got up and walked toward the door. "I've met him a few times. Look, I've got things to do. See what you can come up with. The commission on something like that would be nothing short of a windfall."

"Hey . . . you aren't going to desert me on this are you, Laura? I was counting on your advice."

"No. I'll do what I can. You might as well start going through the multiple listing records and see what you can come up with. I'll get back to you in a little while." She went into her office and closed the door behind her.

Nan didn't have time to puzzle over Laura's odd behavior. She had promised to call Craig Martindale after lunch. There was a multitude of work to be done before then if she were going to come up with a rental property keyed to his particular needs.

*   *   *

Lunchtime came and went. Laura finally emerged from her office in time for an appointment with a young couple looking for a duplex in the Homewood area. When she came out to get a bundle of brochures from the storage cabinet she stopped at Nan's desk. "Any ideas yet?"

Nan shook her head. "When Fred came in a little while ago, I asked him to keep his eyes open for a ski lodge that might fit the rental requirements, but he couldn't think of a thing offhand. Betty is still out with her client."

Nan brushed her copper-colored hair from her face. "I hope she wraps up the sale on that townhouse over at Stateline."

"She needs it, that's for sure. Listen, Nan, my first reaction when you told me about Craig Martindale was that you had bitten off more than you could chew. Well, if it were anyone else but you, I might believe that, but even though it's a monumental undertaking, I have the feeling you can handle it."

Nan was surprised. "I appreciate your confidence, Laura. I'll do the best I can."

"Think positively. We'll come up with something if it kills us."

Nan attempted a grin. "Which it very well might."

The other couple in the office was becoming restless. Laura smiled at Nan and waggled her fingers. "Talk to you later."

Nan reached for the telephone and started calling the list of names she had written down. They were, for the most part, old family connections from the time when her father was Assistant District Attorney for Tahoe County. He had been dead now for seven years; killed when his car had skidded off the road near Carnelian Bay during a sleet storm. Her mother had died just six months ago . . . but she didn't want to think about that now, she couldn't, not on top of everything else.

The tenth name on her list was Judge Quincy, whom she hadn't seen since her father's funeral. He had given her little encouragement but the one name he had suggested left her too distracted to continue her calls.

Robert Easton. The name rang like a clarion inside her head, calling up memories of the less-than-happy days when she was in high school. His face flashed before her now—wide-set deep brown eyes fringed with gold-tipped lashes, thick brown hair shot with red-gold highlights from summers spent on the lake, a finely chiseled mouth set in a square jaw that warned of an inner stubbornness. For Nan he had been the epitome of masculinity during her high-school days.

He was a college man then, four years older than she. Pursued by cheerleaders, prom queens, he dated the best, or at least the most popular.

That was why it came as a shock when he asked her to the dance after the game with State. True, it was something of a fad in those days for college men to date high-school seniors, but they didn't date just any seniors. Certainly not the ones who looked like Nan did at that time, unless they happened to be wealthy like Mitzi MacIntyre, whose dad let her dates drive his Rolls Royce.

Nan had been thin, colorless, and painfully shy where boys were concerned. She was an excellent student, but when it came to social functions she retreated within herself. Most of the boys who made any attempt at all to date her did so because they wanted her to tutor them in whatever subject they were trying to bone up on. She knew what they were doing, and accepted it because there was little she could do about it.

But Robert Easton didn't need tutoring. Along with his money, his charm, and social prestige, he had more than his share of intelligence, a fact which put him at the head of his class.

When he asked Nan to the dance that September so many years ago, she felt that for the first time in her life there was nothing left for her to pray for. She had it all. Her mother had tried to warn her that the Eastons of this world breathed more rarified air than people like the Gilliams. She told Nan it was a mistake to try to cross their social barriers. Not that the Gilliams were poor; they just weren't rich. She had laughed and called her mother old fashioned, resenting what she thought was her attempt to dampen Nan's happiness.

It was only later, when she entered the Regency Room at the hotel with her hand on Robert's arm, that she realized how right her mother had been.

She tried hard to pull her thoughts back to the present. The couple had just come out of Laura's office. Apparently she

hadn't fared too well with them. Laura was a first-class real
estate broker. She knew her business from top to bottom, but
between the high cost of housing, the skyrocketing interest
rates, and the determination of the local people to halt the
incredibly rapid growth of the Tahoe area, she sometimes felt
as if she were fighting a losing battle.

Laura saw the people to the door and made sure they had
her business card with her home phone number on it, then
walked over to Nan's desk and sank down in a chair. "So how
goes it? Have you been able to come up with a promising
lead?"

"Not a one."

Laura glanced over at the pad and saw the name Robert
Easton scrawled a half dozen times over the page. Nan saw
her gaze at the page and offered, "I knew him a long time ago.
You must know of him; he's head of Easton Enterprises."

Laura let out a slow whistle. "Of course. Now you're talking
money. They own the lion's share of the political pie in this
county, not to mention half the real estate. How do you happen
to know him?"

"It's a long story."

Laura cocked her head.

Nan shrugged. "I don't want to go into it now, but maybe
sometime I'll tell you all about it. At present he's the owner
of the kind of place we're looking for, but the chances are one
in a million that he would even consider talking about renting
it."

"So call him and find out."

"Not yet. I'm not quite that desperate."

Laura got up. "Okay. I bow to your judgment, but time is
fast slipping away. We can't afford to lose this deal, Nan."
The blond woman turned at the doorway. "By the way, your
'ex' called a while ago. I told him you were on another line."

"Did he say what he wanted?"

Laura shrugged. "Nope. But then he never did like me since
the time I told him to grow up and stop trying to kill himself
with his schoolboy antics. What's he up to now? Is it hang-
gliding or auto racing or something new?"

"I really don't know. It's been a month or so since I saw
him. He was still trying to get his racer into the time trials."

"Well, if you're lucky you've seen the last of him. You were nothing but a bundle of nerves just before your divorce. It's good to see you finally able to relax."

Nan laughed. "I don't think I'll have much time to relax until I find a lodge for our Mr. Martindale."

Laura grinned as she turned and went into her own office. Nan's gaze returned to the name she had scrawled on the pad. Robert Easton. She had hated him for so long. Could she face him again after all these years . . . after what she did to him that night? She ran her tongue over her lips to get rid of the dryness. As surely as she knew tomorrow would come, she knew there was no other way.

Even though it had happened over six years ago, the incident was still as real to her as if it had happened yesterday. When they had entered the ballroom of the hotel that night, just the mere fact that she was his date had given her the measure of confidence she needed to keep her legs from buckling. But they had been there less than ten minutes when they were surrounded by a group of laughing fraternity men who began stuffing bills into Robert's pockets.

A pimply-faced beanpole had brought a sack full of pennies which he proceeded to dump in a pile on the floor. "I've gotta give you credit, man," he said. "I never thought you'd have the nerve to bring her. There it is, ten bucks, and you sure as hell earned every cent of it." He grinned as he dropped the empty bag onto the pile.

As the truth of why Robert had invited her to the dance dawned on her, hurt mixed with anger until it was all she could do to hold back the tears. Summoning all the courage she possessed, she laughed in the boy's face and told him he had wasted his money. She had been in on the joke from the beginning. That was a lie, of course, but it had been the only way to save face. As she looked up at Robert she thought she saw a spark of admiration in his eyes, but it soon died when he saw the expression on her face. Once they were alone she turned on him with blind fury. To this day she remembered her words. "God help me, you'll pay for this, Robert Easton, if it takes till the day I die."

Remembering the encounter now, she felt perspiration bead

her upper lip. It was Betty Lemmer, back from her tour of homes, who finally managed to drag Nan back to the present. She leaned over Nan's desk, her blond hair swinging like a frazzled rope in the wind.

"Hey, Nan, Laura told me you were in a bind, but I didn't think it was *that* bad." She motioned to the paper on which Nan had been doodling.

Nan looked down. She had written "God help me" in six different places on the pad. The heat began to rise in her face, but she made an effort to laugh it off. "If Laura told you what my client is looking for then you should know I'll need all the help I can get."

Betty sat down on the corner of her desk. "She did, and I see your point. Have you come up with anything at all?"

Nan looked at her watch. "Not really. And I have only about ten minutes in which to make up my mind before I have to call Los Angeles."

"So what's the problem? Tell him you've got several leads and are checking them out. If you can't, it's still no big deal. Sure he'll be mad, but what can he do from Los Angeles?"

"That's not the point, Betty. It's a question of integrity."

"Integrity-smegrity. This is the real estate business, for pete's sake. You've got to take a gamble once in a while. Laura's counting on you not to let her down."

Betty's parting thrust did it. Nan was fiercely loyal to Laura since the day Laura had taken her on as a fledgling agent before the ink was even dry on her certificate. Nan had desperately needed a job to help pay for Lance's hospital bills after his accident in the demolition derby. Even though Nan considered herself worthy of that trust as she progressed in the business, she still felt a sense of obligation.

As the hand on the clock clicked out the hour of two, she lifted the receiver and dialed Craig Martindale's number in Los Angeles. It took him several minutes to get to the phone, a fact which irritated Nan because he should have been expecting her call.

He didn't waste time with preliminaries. "So what have you got for me?"

She swallowed. "Nothing definite as yet, but I have some

calls to make this afternoon which should be productive."

"Look, lady. Let's lay it on the top line. Can you get me a place or can't you?"

Nan felt her back stiffen. "My name is Gilliam, Nan Gilliam. I can tell you this, Mr. Martindale. I'm doing my very best. If it is possible for anyone to find the kind of place you're looking for at Lake Tahoe, I'll find it for you."

She could almost hear his grin over the phone. "Well now, that's all I ask. Get back to me this time tomorrow." With that he hung up and Nan found herself staring at the telephone receiver she still held in her hand.

Her legs weren't quite steady when she went into Laura's office. "Well, I'm in up to my neck. I as good as told him I could find what he wants. I always believed in making things happen. I hope I haven't dug us into the proverbial hole."

Laura rubbed one hand across the top of the other, staring at the faint liver spots which freckled her skin. "You and me both, Nan. You and me both." She paused for a moment as if weighing their chances, then looked up. "What the hell?" She laughed. "This is Tahoe, the most beautiful gambling town on earth. What are we doing here if we can't afford to take a few chances now and then?"

An hour before Nan was ready to go home that night, the prospects looked worse rather than better. Even with the whole team concentrating their efforts to find a vacant lodge, they came up blank. The one or two places which seemed to remotely fill the bill were owned by people who were scandalized at the idea of renting to moviemakers. At four-thirty Nan yielded to the inevitable and called Easton Enterprises.

Chapter Two

THE SMOOTH VOICE of the secretary tried valiantly to lull Nan into a sense of security. "I'm sorry, Mr. Easton is unavailable at the moment, but if you would care to leave your name I'm sure he will call you at his earliest convenience."

Nan realized it was a dodge. He obviously received dozens of unwanted calls during the day. If he recognized her name he would never return the call. She swallowed and took a deep breath. One thing for sure, he wouldn't know the name Nan Hendricks. She had never asked anything from Lance in the past, the least he could do is let her borrow his name for an emergency. She assumed her most efficient, businesslike voice. "This is Nan Hendricks from Pinnacle Realty. I have a matter of the utmost importance to discuss with Mr. Easton. Can you set up an appointment for me with him tomorrow?"

"Could you tell me the nature of the business, Ms. Hendricks?"

"I'm sorry. Mr. Easton has not given me permission to disclose the information to anyone as yet."

"Oh, I see. Forgive me, Ms. Hendricks. I didn't mean to pry, but you see we get so many opportunists on the telephone. If you could be here at one tomorrow, Mr. Easton has a few minutes between appointments. Will it take very long?"

"I don't believe so. One o'clock will be fine. Thank you very much."

Nan barely had time to replace the receiver before Laura, Betty, and Fred swarmed around her desk. Betty grinned. "Handled like an old pro if I do hate to admit it. Keep it up, gal, and you'll become real competition."

Later, as she drove home, Nan wished she felt as good about the appointment as they did. Of course, they didn't know the background of her acquaintance with Robert Easton, so they couldn't know or begin to understand her reluctance to see him.

She was bone tired and would liked to have spent the next hour soaking in a hot tub, but as if to top off the day, Lance was waiting on her doorstep when she arrived home. He grinned boyishly as he saw her approach.

Pulling the car into the narrow drive in front of the redwood-planked house, Nan got out and slammed the door, then walked toward her former husband where he leaned against the stone wall. She dug in her bag for the key. "What are you doing here, Lance?"

He shrugged. "I had a couple of errands to run. I thought maybe you'd like to go to dinner and the show. Rich Little is our headliner this week. I know he's your favorite comedian. After I get off work we could maybe take a drive and watch the sun come up over the lake."

She made a face. "Be serious."

He took the key from her and unlocked the door, then motioned her to precede him into the house. She looked at him and shook her head. "Nice try, Lance. Give me the key," she said as she held out her hand.

"Win a few, lose a few." He laughed and returned her key. "What's for dinner?"

"Honesty pudding and faithful pie," she said. "But knowing you, neither of them would agree with your digestion, so you'd better just leave. I know you have plenty to do before show time. You can't afford to be late."

"I've got plenty of time. There's no rush. I'm the best emcee they ever had at the Golden Slipper Club. They can't get along without me."

He came closer and rubbed his knuckles across her cheek. "Besides, nothing's more important than seeing you. I never should have let you go."

"Look, I'm not interested. All I want from you is your absence. If you really want to do something for me, leave me alone. Don't call me, don't come to see me...just stay out of my life."

He came to stand behind her and put his arms around her shoulders. "You can't put an end to our feelings just by signing a couple of papers. Don't forget, babes, we shared some pretty good times in there." He nodded toward the bedroom. "Don't tell me you don't miss it after such a long dry spell."

She felt the familiar warmth flood through her veins. It *had* been a long time. She had been a virgin until she married Lance. After that it was as if all the desires she had suppressed for a lifetime had been released. Marriage was the natural state for her. She needed to have the comfort of a man's arms around her, to feel the heat of his desire in tandem with hers. But now her instinct told her it wasn't Lance whom she needed, because he had always left her feeling less than complete.

Abruptly she pulled away. "I'm telling you for the last time, Lance. Don't ever come back here. It's over. I don't want to see you again."

"I had you going there for a minute, didn't I?" He smiled as he turned and walked toward the front door. "Actually, there was another reason I stopped by to see you but I don't suppose you're interested."

"Not really."

"Your loss. I was going to cut you in on a good thing. I'm working on a system to beat the odds at the blackjack table."

She rolled her eyes heavenward. "Don't tell me you've started gambling?"

"It's no gamble when you've got a sure thing. All I have to do is get a little capital together and I'll be ready to show them a thing or two."

"Goodbye, Lance."

He grinned. "So long, babes. Sorry I can't stay for dinner, but you know how it is."

She followed him to make sure he actually left. He liked to play games. She wouldn't have put it past him to slam the door and only pretend to leave.

It took her a while to settle down after he was gone. Lance had awakened desires she had thought were deeply buried. Angry with herself for even thinking such thoughts, she slipped into a pair of jeans and began to straighten up the house. It was, for the most part, busywork. She lived alone in this three-bedroom house, and it didn't take a great deal of effort to keep it clean. Of course, compared to her mother's standards—which had required that the windows be washed once a week and the sheets changed every day—Nan could hardly call herself an expert housekeeper, but she sensed that her mother would not have been disappointed in her.

Nan had changed few things in the house since the day she had been forced to place her mother in the skilled-care nursing home. The walnut furniture still glowed darkly against the ivory walls. Deep velvet carpeting, the same throughout most of the house, was a subtle shade of gold tempered with a touch of umber. The living room, with its period furniture, was decorated in a lighter gold in the drapes and chairs while the sofa was covered with a sculptured velvet floral pattern in muted shades of rust, green, and persimmon.

The family room, her favorite, was decorated in all the warmth of the colors of the earth. Books lined a wall on each side of the fireplace, bringing back memories of evenings when her parents sat across from each other in silent companionship as they read the classics. Deep lounge chairs in rust velvet faced a wall of glass doors which opened onto a deck overlooking Lake Tahoe. She pulled the drapes open all the way to reveal the full panorama of the late afternoon sun slanting low across the lake. Soon it would sink below the mountain.

Opening the glass doors, she walked onto the redwood deck and leaned against the rail. The scent of pine was everywhere. How she loved this place! Thank God that was one thing Lance hadn't been able to take from her. With the money left in trust she would easily be able to keep up the taxes, even if something should happen to her job.

Thinking about work naturally brought her mind back to the impending appointment with Robert Easton. A small twinge of guilt nagged at her conscience. She wished now she had used her own name and not given his secretary the impression that she was involved with him in a mysterious business deal. Still, the chances were great that either she would never have gotten beyond the secretary or that Robert would have remembered her name and point blank refused to talk to her. No. She had done the only thing possible under the circumstances, and for now she had to live with it. Later on she could mend her fences if things went the way she hoped they would.

Oddly enough, Craig Martindale had been easier to deal with than she had expected. She had been honest with him. She certainly planned to do her very best to find the shooting location he was looking for.

What she needed now was a "wedge," as her father had called it, something to drive in behind her proposal to Robert Easton to make him feel it was to his advantage to accept her offer of a month's rental on his lodge. But what could she offer a man like him, short of putting her head on the chopping block? She laughed mirthlessly. If she did that he would probably *pay* the studio to rent the lodge.

She pounded her fist on the rail. "Darn him," she said aloud. "Why does he always have to get in my way?"

After a quick meal of French onion soup, a half can of tuna emptied over some shredded cabbage, and a quartered orange, she washed her hair, showered, and went to bed with a book.

Call it inspiration or whatever else, but she suddenly remembered her conversation with Kennedy Williams, a contractor for whom her father had done considerable legal work over the years. He, too, had mentioned the Easton lodge as her best possibility of finding a rental for the movie company.

A chance remark about one end of the roof being in need of repair had stuck in her mind. The wedge! She knew it as surely as she knew her own name. If Robert were the kind of businessman everyone claimed he was, he certainly couldn't refuse an offer to have his lodge restored to its natural beauty.

She slammed the book with satisfaction. If her luck held and he didn't remember her, there was a good possibility that Robert Easton would be impressed by her not-too-subtle logic. She squinted as she leaned back and turned off the light. He had to be impressed. If he weren't, she didn't have the slightest idea where to turn next.

A half-hour later, even before the digital clock flipped over to nine-thirty, she was sound asleep from sheer mental exhaustion.

Usually the squirrels scampering across the roof didn't even waken her, but the next morning she was awake at five, an hour and a half early. Slipping into jeans and a sweatshirt, she put on a pair of sneakers and ran down to the lake. A brisk row in her small boat brought the color to her cheeks and created an appalling appetite. She was grateful for the fact that there was no longer enough time to fix a large breakfast, or she might have been tempted to have pancakes, her number-one weakness.

Surprisingly, both Laura and Betty were at the office when she arrived. Fred had gone out early to do an appraisal and wasn't expected in until ten.

"Well, look at her," Betty said, raising an eyebrow. "Here we sit breaking our backs to find you a lodge and you come in a minute and twenty-five seconds late."

Nan laughed, recognizing Betty's abortive attempt at humor. "I hope your dedication has produced something other than spite."

Betty grinned. "Nope! Looks like you're stuck with the Easton Empire. For the life of me I can't see why you're so dead set against talking to them. All they can do is say no, and even then you might make some good contacts. After all, contacts is where it's at in this business."

Nan was saved from having to answer when Laura called her into the office.

"Are you all set for your appointment?" She surveyed Nan from head to toe. "Well, you certainly look ready. That beige linen suit looks smashing, and that tangerine scarf sets it off like it came from Saks Fifth Avenue. If it had been me, I'd have worn costume jewelry with the suit, and it would have looked like the corner dry goods store. That's what I mean about class, Nan. Of course it doesn't hurt a bit that you're tall and slim and have the complexion of a movie star."

She walked over to lean against the door frame as she continued. "It comes to you so naturally. Just like when you talked me out of buying that slick plastic furniture for the office. I thought it looked great until I saw how nice the leather you chose blended with the paneling." She folded her arms across her chest. "So how about it? Have you come to terms with yourself? I know you weren't thrilled with confronting the Easton bunch in regard to the rental, but I don't see any alternative."

Nan shrugged. "I can't say I'm happy about it, but I'll go through with it since there seems to be no other option. Of course it's rather iffy, but I have thought of a few angles which might give us an edge on the contract—providing he doesn't throw me out before I get to talk to him."

About that time the usual Saturday "looky lou's" began tramping into the office, and all the agents were busy answering questions, pointing out locations on the map, and handing out brochures. At twenty of one Nan signaled that she was leaving for her appointment. Laura gave her the victory sign and Betty winked across her desk as Nan took her briefcase and went out the door.

The Easton Annex was a group of high-rise offices in the building adjoining the King Midas Hotel. Nan approved of the sedate black marble facing softened by a row of set-in planter boxes next to the walk. They were filled with multitudes of red geraniums in full bloom. Thanks to the time of day, she was able to park within a half-block of the entrance. Later, the street would be jammed with cars.

A sleek-haired Oriental girl checked her daybook, then cordially directed Nan to a bank of elevators at one end of the room and advised her that Mr. Easton's secretary would be expecting her.

As the elevator whisked her toward the ninth floor, the enormity of what she had done washed over her like an icy shower in the dead of winter. Her stomach began to feel as if she had eaten a box of sunflower seeds. Nerves could apparently produce the same effect as an allergy.

Would he remember her? She just could not go on letting

him think her name was Nan Hendricks. It would be too embarrassing if he found out from someone else who she was.
She glanced at herself in the elevator mirror. Recognize
her. . . . How could he? She no more resembled that shy teenager than a coal miner's shack compared to the Taj Mahal. She
didn't consider herself a beauty, but her curves were all in the
right places and her hair glowed with the sheen of antique
copper. She lifted her chin. It had been six years since she had
seen him. Even wounded pride must heal in that length of time.
The knowledge gave her just the assurance she needed as she
stepped off the elevator and into the world of high finance.

"Ms. Hendricks? Good morning. I'm Claudia Mansfield,
Mr. Easton's private secretary. Will you sit down, please? Mr.
Easton will see you in just a few minutes. May I get you a cup
of coffee?"

"Thank you, no. I'll just look at a magazine."

She picked up a copy of *Fortune* and tried to focus her eyes
on a page but was infinitely aware of the appraisal she was
being given by Ms. Mansfield. The older woman with the
champagne-silver hair was completely incapable of concealing
her curiosity.

A chime rang once and echoed for a bare two seconds. If
a sound could be described as iridescent this would surely be
a fitting example.

The secretary rose. "Mr. Easton will see you now, Ms.
Hendricks. Will you come this way, please?"

Nan followed her down a short, thickly carpeted corridor
to the office at the end of the hall.

"Mr. Easton, Ms. Hendricks is here." She backed away and
closed the door behind her.

Nan felt as if her heart was stuck in her throat. Gone was
all her newly acquired self-assurance. Standing before her, a
quizzical smile tugging at the corner of his mouth, was Robert
Easton. He was the same boy she had known, grown older of
course, with a touch of gray at the temples and a stunning
mustache which did nothing to detract from his appearance.
She wanted desperately to sit down, but he came forward and
extended his hand.

"How do you do, Ms. Hendricks. You must forgive me,

but my secretary seems to think we have some very important business pending. Have I missed something along the way?"

He was still holding her hand in his firm grip as Nan edged away. It was the same Robert Easton, all right. She would have recognized that amused tolerance anywhere. The question which bothered Nan was . . . Did he recognize her?

Chapter Three

WHEN SHE WAS finally able to retrieve her hand Nan also recovered a degree of composure. She straightened her shoulders and forced a smile. "I'm afraid I owe you an apology, Mr. Easton. To begin, my name is no longer Hendricks. It's Gilliam, Nan Gilliam." She went on quickly in the hope that the name would mean nothing to him. "Also, I confess to deliberately misleading your secretary because I felt it was the only way I could manage to get an appointment with you on such short notice."

He gave a dry, humorless laugh. "Believe me, you aren't the first, Mrs. Gilliam. I assume congratulations are in order, accounting for your change in name."

Nan looked blank and then it dawned on her that he assumed she was a bride. "I suppose there are some who might think so, but I have recently divorced. It's Miss Gilliam, not Mrs."

He looked slightly embarrassed. "Well, since you are here,

why don't we sit down while you tell me why you wanted to talk to me."

She reached into her bag and produced one of her business cards. "I'm with Pinnacle Realty. A client of mine from Los Angeles is desperately in need of a mountain-lodge setting in which to film a portion of a movie. Your lodge up at Tahoe Mountain is the only location I have been able to find which would adequately fill all his requirements."

He threw his head back and laughed. "You've got to be joking. Before I'd let..."

She held up her hand. "Don't say no until I tell you the rest of it. You're a businessman, Mr. Easton, and I have a proposition for you that you won't be able to pass up."

His left eyebrow rose a good half-inch as he motioned with his hand. "Go on."

"I'm sure you know what dry rot is. That's what you have on your roof. You know the old pine tree that overhangs the house?"

He nodded as she continued.

"Every time there's a storm, the snow collects under the branches of the tree and doesn't melt along with the rest of the snow. Consequently, it stays on the cedar shakes, never permitting them to really dry out until late in the spring. Considering the amount of antique furniture you have in the house, I would think you'd be concerned about the chances of a leak in the roof."

She paused to judge his reaction, but he just sat there watching her. She took a deep breath. "Of course if someone were living there it would be less risky, but if you have only opened the house twice in the last five years, there's no telling what might have happened to the furniture."

His eyes lit up with amusement. "Anything else?"

"Just this. What you really need is a new roof, just on the south wing, of course, and someone to prune the big tree to prevent further damage. Simply by leasing the house for a month, you could have the entire job done at no cost to you."

"My dear Miss Gilliam, do you have any idea what havoc a crew of movie people can wreak on a house in a month's time?"

"That would certainly be a consideration. The studio would

naturally be required to post a bond. Your own attorney could draw up the lease if that would allay your fears."

He tapped a pencil on his desk. "I don't think you realize what you're asking of me. Just when were you last up there?"

Nan chewed at her lower lip. "Truthfully, I've never been up to your lodge. The information came from a building contractor who is a friend of the family. He is quite familiar with the property."

He grinned. "You could have lied and I probably would have believed you." He looked at his watch. "Let's take a ride up there."

She gulped then stood up. "All right. May I call my office before we leave?"

He pushed the phone over to her. "Dial nine for an outside line."

Nan was grateful that Robert Easton couldn't hear the other end of the conversation. When Laura heard that they were driving up to the lodge, she let out a whoop. "Hallelujah! Anyone else he would have thrown out. I have a feeling this is in the bag."

Nan tried to keep her voice calm. "If I'm not back by two would you please call Los Angeles and tell my client that I'm working on his rental and will get back to him as soon as possible? You'll find his number on the Rolodex on my desk." Thanking Laura, she hung up.

Robert Easton, who had spoken to his secretary during the phone conversation, was already at the door. "Did you drive?" he asked.

"Yes. I parked down the block."

"Good. We'll go in your car instead of the limousine, if that's all right with you."

A short time later, he waited until she unlocked the car, then seated her and closed the door. It took a little maneuvering for him to fit his long legs under the dash but he did so, then rested his arm along the back of the seat.

"The best way to get there is to take Route 50 to Emerald Bay Road. Make a right, then make a left at Fallen Leaf Road and another left at Tahoe Mountain Road." As she nodded he settled back against the seat.

Nan stole a surreptitious glance now and then in an attempt

to judge his mood. If he remembered her name and their past association, he gave no outward sign of it. He appeared completely at ease with her driving, unlike Lance who constantly nagged at her to change lanes, speed up, or slow down. Despite her case of nerves, Nan found herself enjoying the day as if it were an outing.

The air was cool and brilliantly clear, the lake like blue crystal. Once away from the Nevada border, the demarcation line for the gambling casinos, the traffic thinned considerably, permitting Nan to relax and enjoy the scenery. It never failed to thrill her. The Sierra Nevada Mountains, sprinkled with golden aspen amid the green of the pine trees, rose sharply upward to meet the endless sky. Fallen Leaf Road was all but deserted. They met an occasional camper-trailer, but except in rare places the blacktop road was wide enough to accommodate both vehicles.

Despite her efforts to concentrate on her driving, Robert Easton's overwhelming masculinity kept intruding on her senses. But oddly, he wore his maleness unconsciously, a fact which made it all the more intriguing. Where Lance would have been flaunting himself and coming on to her, Robert Easton could as easily have been riding with his attorney. It suddenly occurred to her that maybe he didn't find her attractive enough to waste his time. The thought rankled and she stepped on the gas and honked as she went around a tourist, rubbernecking as he passed a particularly beautiful spot. Robert Easton turned toward her with an amused expression, then looked away.

Finally they turned off onto a narrow blacktop road marked at the entrance by a huge boulder topped with a bronze globe held in the claws of a giant eagle. The globe bore a narrow plaque with the name Easton emblazoned in black letters. The lane was bordered on each side with pine trees, close set with straight dark trunks rising spirelike toward the sky. A thick carpet of needles, pungent and dry, appeared to have lain undisturbed for a decade or more.

As they rounded a rocky outcropping, a stag sprang onto the road and made for the other side. Nan wrenched the wheel to the right and then to the left in an effort to avoid hitting the deer. Robert Easton, caught unaware, was thrown against her

so violently that he had to reach behind her to the opposite side
of the car to keep from hurting her.

"Oh my gosh!" she exclaimed. "Are you all right? It happened so fast I didn't have a chance to think."

He laughed. "I'd say you thought rather quickly. Most drivers would have hit the deer. The question is, are *you* all right?
I'm afraid I nearly fell on top of you."

"I'm fine." She laughed nervously, hoping that he would
consider the fact that she was shaking, an aftermath of their
near-accident instead of the result of the sudden contact of his
arm with the top of her shoulders. He had removed it rather
slowly, a fact which did little to relieve her tendency toward
breathlessness.

It was becoming increasingly harder to maintain the fine
degree of hatred she had generated toward Robert Easton since
her school days. Sitting next to her, he exuded an aura of
confidence in himself and complete satisfaction with the way
he was running his life. At the same time he was attentive to
her conversation and appeared to respect her opinions.

Rounding a curve, the lodge sprang into full view. It was
of redwood construction, as might be expected, with a pair of
two-story wings set at angles to each other. Centered in the V
was a mammoth geodesic dome constructed of native stone,
redwood, and glass. It nestled among the trees as if it were a
part of the earth itself.

Nan guided the car onto the semicircular drive and drew to
a halt in front of the tall doors which marked the entrance.
Almost before she turned off the ignition, Robert Easton had
jumped out of the car and gone around to open her door.

"Well, this is it. After your concern for my roof I'm glad
to see that it hasn't fallen down."

Nan looked at his face to be sure that he was teasing. He
was. Nevertheless, her face turned bright pink. She gave a
defiant flip to her hair. "So you were lucky. How long your
luck can hold out is another question. Once the roof leaks, it's
too late to save the furnishings."

It was a strange feeling to be walking alongside him as they
approached the front door and paused while he turned the key
in the lock, then motioned for her to enter. The sensation was
so domestic that she had to talk quickly to cover her case of

nerves. "I had no idea that the geodesic dome would be a part of the architectural plan. It's absolutely fabulous."

"Buckminster Fuller was a friend of my father. He was the designer of the original domes, and it was his contention that a dome is the most economical, energy-efficient structure available. He said that every time you double the size of a geodesic dome you achieve eight times as much volume while adding only four times as much external surface."

"Did he design this dome?"

"No. Just the original concept which was patented in 1954. But many of his ideas were incorporated into this one." He followed her inside and closed the door behind him. They had stepped into an extraordinarily large room with vaulted ceilings that arched their way to a circle of glass at the top of the dome. Along one wall a narrow stairway led to a wide balcony on which Nan could see lounge chairs, a sofa, and bookshelves. To one side there was a small table which appeared to be a game table for chess or checkers.

But it was the main floor which held her attention. A great stone fireplace, open on all sides, dominated the area to the left. The rear wall of the dome was glass; curved sections of windows that looked out over absolute paradise. A pair of sliding glass doors opened onto a deck, but beyond that there was not another vestige of civilization for as far as she could see. Far below, beyond the woods and valleys filled with wild-flower meadows, was Lake Tahoe, shimmering in a blue haze. She turned to face him. "How could you possibly stay away from here? If it were mine I'd never want to leave."

He shrugged. "A question of economics. Besides, the place is too large for a single man. It needs a family."

"Are you planning to sell it?"

He grinned. "Ah yes, for a moment I had forgotten you are a real estate person. No, I don't plan to sell. I may eventually live up here, but for now . . ."

Nan, feeling as if she had intruded into his private life, turned away and began a cursory inspection of the main room.

Dust sheets covered most of the furniture. As Robert Easton walked over to one side of the room and pulled away several of the shroudlike coverings, her gaze was drawn to the space between the huge upright beams which were divided into hexagonal shapes of uniform size. A giant sunburst mural made of thousands of pieces of ceramic tile filled an entire hexagon from floor to ceiling. The colors darkened from a vibrant yellow at the center through shades of gold, orange, red, and rust as they radiated outward. It was a striking contrast to the dark wood paneling and the gold, brown, and rust tweed carpet.

She heard him chuckle as he ran his hand over a fine Queen Anne table. "No water damage so far, but they could use a good polish."

Nan moved across the room. "Is that really a Henry the Eighth desk?" she asked. "It must be worth a fortune."

"Probably. And that's just one of the reasons it would be foolish to lease this place. The lodge has a great many antiques. Can you imagine what a film crew would do to it?"

Nan was beginning to have her own doubts. "My client told me that they would be bringing only a minimum crew on location, but I can understand why you would hesitate. On the other hand, if you look at it as an expanding investment, the value of the house itself can only go up if a successful movie is filmed here. It's a matter of prestige. People enjoy the vicarious thrill of owning a house which was chosen as a movie location."

He nodded. "Of course that would pay off only if I intended to sell the house, which I don't." He gestured toward a stairway near the rear of the dome. "Would you like to go downstairs?"

"Certainly. I hadn't realized there was another floor."

"There is just a portion of a floor fitted into the side of the hill, but I think you'll find it rather interesting."

Fascinating might have been a better word. Nan turned to look at him. "Is that really what it looks like . . . a trout stream flowing right through the room?"

"I can't vouch for the number of trout in it these days, but yes, it's a natural stream which flows down out of the mountains. As you can see, it's nearly dry this time of the year, but in the spring the snow melt fills that basin to the brim." He motioned to a door behind him. "That leads to the sauna. For those who like to follow a steambath with a dip in an icy pool, everything is right at hand. Of course the heat is turned off now because there is no one here to use it."

She walked over to one side, where tiers of stone benches

circling a hot tub appeared to be carved into the wall. A brilliant array of pads and pillows were scattered at random and overhead an intricate series of lights provided artificial suns to warm as well as tan.

She laughed. "Everything but sand to get into your eyes."

He grinned. "Well, we do our best, but there are some luxuries we have to forego." He took her arm. "Would you like to see the bedrooms and suites in the adjoining wings?"

"I . . ." She hesitated, then nodded. "I don't believe the shooting schedule requires bedrooms but I might as well see what you have to offer." The minute it was out she could have bitten her tongue. It had sounded so . . . suggestive. "I mean . . ."

He threw his head back and laughed. "You don't have to explain. I know what you mean."

Darn him! Why couldn't he have let it pass? She silently fumed. She was angry enough she could have hit him. The sensation brought back a flood of memories of that night in the middle of the dance floor and her face crimsoned. He apparently assumed he had embarrassed her and he laughed again.

"On second thought, why don't we leave the bedrooms to another time?" He looked at his watch. "I have an appointment later this afternoon, so perhaps we should be on our way." He handed her the keys. "If you don't mind I'll go out the side door and check things around in back while you lock up the front."

"Fine. I'll meet you at the car."

Less than five minutes later he came striding around the corner of the house. Nan was impressed with his athletic grace and his superb build. And his gray suit with dark gray patches on the elbows worn with a darker gray turtleneck sweater looked as much at home in his elegant office as it did here in this sylvan setting. He got in and closed the door firmly behind him as Nan started the engine.

The trip back to his office was accomplished in what seemed like no time at all. He had as yet to give any indication of his feelings about leasing the lodge, and she was determined not to press him. Hard sell had never been her method of operation, and she was sure that Robert Easton would only resist such tactics.

But when they arrived at the office complex and he still

hadn't mentioned a decision, she began to get a little edgy. Did he expect her to accompany him to his office or was her allotted time finished? As she pulled into a space in front of the building he made no move to get out but sat there looking at her.

She put her foot on the emergency brake and shifted into neutral. "Have you had enough time to consider my offer, Mr. Easton? I hesitate to rush you, but time is one of the important elements in this transaction."

"I appreciate your not wanting to rush me. When someone tries to push a deal through too quickly, I always find it suspect." He seemed to be waiting for something.

Finally, she turned toward him. "May I give you a call in the morning?"

He had the strangest expression on his face. "The first thing you can give me is my key ring."

Her face turned bright red as she scrambled for her handbag, at the same time remembering how she felt when Lance had kept *her* keys. "I . . . I'm terribly sorry. It was force of habit, I guess. I just shoved them into my purse."

He held his hand out, waiting. In exasperation she dumped the contents of her purse on the seat and found them entangled with her wallet. As she handed him the keys her fingers brushed his palm, sending a tremor of electricity through her. She glanced up to see if he had noticed. He had, and the knowledge infuriated her.

She pulled herself up straight in the seat and looked him in the eyes. "Well, Mr. Easton, have you come to a decision?"

"I'd like more time to think about it. Shall we discuss it over dinner tonight?"

Her first impulse was to refuse. The gong sounding in her brain warned her that she was getting into water over her head. The last time he had asked her for a date was nothing less than a disaster. Would it be any different this time? Then she had been lucky enough to get off with injured pride, but something told her there was much more at stake now. And that was the problem. Her job was also on the line. The contract could mean a great deal to her career, so much that she couldn't take a chance on losing it. After all, she was the "brightest young dynamo to grace the real estate business in the last ten years," according to the local newspaper. She ought to be able to handle just about anything. Nan grinned as she remembered the flowery phrases.

"Sure. Dinner it is. May I call for you at your hotel?"

He smiled. "No. That would be carrying women's liberation a little far. I'll pick you up at seven. I assume that was your home address on your business card. We'll have dinner at Harrahs if that appeals to you."

She nodded. "Whatever you say. I'll expect you at seven."

He gave a mock salute and, turning, strode into his building.

Nan was still in a state of numbness when she arrived back at the office. Somehow she managed to get through the rest of the day. Fred and Betty were convinced that she had the deal wrapped up, but Laura made a valiant effort to remain cautious. A call to Craig Martindale in Los Angeles only served to fuel Nan's feeling of uneasiness. He seemed so certain of her ability to fulfill his needs and Nan, of course, had to maintain a façade of confidence in front of her client, but she wondered what she would do if Robert Easton turned her down.

Going out to dinner with him was the last thing in the world she wanted to do. He was way out of her class. True, her family background was upper middle class, but that was still a far cry from the Palm Beach/Riviera set. As she stood in front of the full-length mirror and surveyed her reflection she mentally shook herself. It was foolish trying to make something of this date. It was a business meeting, nothing else. Considering her previous luck where Robert Easton was concerned, he might even ask her to pay for his dinner.

She changed clothes three times before she finally settled on a pale gold bouclé, floor-length dress. While it was fancy enough for the nicest supper club, its nubby texture removed it from the "too dressy" category. A trio of gold chains stopped short of the bateau neckline and she selected a short-sleeved cashmere jacket to top it off.

He arrived promptly at seven in a sleek looking silver-gray car which Nan identified immediately as a gas-guzzler.

"You look lovely, Miss Gilliam. I think it's about time that we called each other by our first names, don't you?"

"Yes, if you like." She settled her skirt around her legs as he closed the door of the car. Dressed as he was in a dinner jacket, he reminded her so much of the Robert Easton she had hated . . . and had a crush on . . . so many years ago, that it was all she could do to keep her hands from shaking.

Dinner passed without a hitch. The pressed duck was excellent, as was the watercress salad with just a hint of lemon and ginger. It wasn't until he asked her to dance that she felt her control begin to slip. As they walked onto the floor he looked down at her and began to put his arm around her for one of the slow, traditional dances. For the barest instant he hesitated as if he remembered another dance floor, but then the music soared and he guided her into the dance.

All through dinner she had tried to steer the conversation toward the rental agreement but he always managed to sidestep. By ten she was getting desperate. There was so little time. If she didn't come through with a contract from him there was no other alternative.

Finally she glanced at her watch. "It's been a lovely evening, but I think I'd better be going home. Tomorrow is another work day for me."

He nodded and she was grateful that he didn't protest. She was also grateful that he paid the check because it was just short of astronomical. As they left town he pulled the car into the outside lane and cruised along at a leisurely pace. He was strangely quiet as if he had something on his mind. A short time later he pulled the car into an overlook above Emerald Bay and turned off the motor.

Nan glanced at him in surprise. Surely he wasn't the type to park in the moonlight like some sex-starved teenager. He put his arm along the back of the seat and stared at her as if seeing her for the first time.

"Now then, Nan Gilliam," he said as he reached for her. "I believe we have a long-standing score to settle between us."

Chapter Four

NAN COULD BARELY see his face in the moonlight, but the glint in his eyes left no doubt in her mind that he meant business. She fought for composure.

"I . . . I don't have the slightest idea what you mean."

"The devil you don't. I thought there was something unusual about you the moment you walked into my office. Then tonight when we started to dance, I was convinced I was right. Nan Gilliam . . ." He spat out the words. "I didn't think I'd ever forget that name. You're the only person on earth who has dared to threaten me." His laughter grated harshly in his throat. "No wonder you gave my secretary your married name. You knew I'd never let you get past the elevator door if I'd known who you were."

His hands reached for her shoulders and he pulled her toward him. Nan was appalled at his strength as he nearly lifted her from the seat. She pushed against him with all her might, but he laughed again.

"Now's your chance, Nan. You vowed you'd make me pay for what I did to you. Just what do you plan to do about it?"

His mouth came down over hers with crushing force, bruising her lips against her teeth. She tried to scream but only succeeded in making strangled noises. As she drew her arm back to hit him he grabbed her wrist and forced her down against the seat until she was half prone. His face was tight, his eyes glittered with dangerous fires. "Don't press your luck."

She forced herself to lie still but her breath was coming in ragged gasps and she was certain he could feel the pounding of her heart through the thin fabric of her dress. He was staring at her, his eyes wide and glazed, his breath unsteady. She could feel the strength of his body as he held her down by brute force.

Nan shook her head mutely as tears began to form at the back of her eyelids. He blinked once and slowly eased the pressure against her wrist. As she watched, he lowered his face to hers and kissed her warm and full on the mouth. There was no hatred this time, only a burning excitement that began to build between them as he explored her mouth, probing, tasting, until she felt her bones begin to liquefy.

Suddenly he sat up and moved away from her. With a quick intake of breath she found her evening bag, slid across the seat, opened the door, got out of the car, and ran down the road as if all the demons of hell were after her. If she had expected him to get out and chase her, she was wrong. A brief look of surprise had crossed his face, but afterward he sat there and watched her go. When she turned once to look back he was still sitting there watching.

It was only a short distance to her house. Once her heart stopped pounding she managed to get her breath under control and straighten her gown. She was less than a block away when she heard the car. There was no mistaking the powerful growl of the motor and she turned quickly, ready to start running for help. He was a good distance behind her, coasting along at a speed apparently intended to match her pace but not to catch up with her. Nevertheless she began to run. She *had* to get inside the house before he caught up with her. Heaven only knew what he might do if he managed to get there first.

But her fears were groundless. It was obvious that he had no intention of coming after her. Strangely, it seemed as if his only concern was that she arrive home safely. With trembling hands she yanked open her bag and extracted the key to the front door.

"Oh God," she whispered, and it sounded like an entreaty. The key wouldn't go in. She tried again, flipping the key over and then back. Finally it slipped in and she turned the lock, then opened the door and ducked inside, slamming the door behind her.

For an instant her knees threatened to give way but she grabbed onto the table beside the door and leaned over to peer through the window. The house was dark and she knew he couldn't see her. His car was parked at the end of her drive. His lights were off but she could see the shadowy outline of his form behind the wheel. He waited. She watched. It seemed like an eternity passed. Finally she sighed and turned on the light. As if that were a prearranged signal, Robert eased the car into gear and slowly drove away.

Sinking down into a chair Nan let herself go limp. She was safe. He wouldn't bother her again. Her dress clung to her with the sticky dampness of perspiration. Groaning, she pushed herself out of the chair and went into the bedroom to undress and shower.

The water was warm and soothing, caressing her body until each nerve end was alive and expectant. She closed her eyes tightly, then leaned her arms against the tile wall and rested her head on her wrists. One thought kept returning no matter how hard she tried to suppress it. She had wanted him. With all the sensations born of three years of marriage, her body ached with a need that nothing else could satisfy. She was like a wanderer on a desert, too long denied a cooling drink, only to have it promised, then taken away.

With an angry motion she gave the handle a whack and turned the cold water on full blast until the icy needles stung her spine. Breathless at last, she pulled on a gown and crawled into bed with the hope of losing herself in sleep.

It wasn't until the next morning that she thought about the lease for the lodge. The toast eased out of the toaster with the tantalizing odor of warm pumpernickel and caraway seeds. Without stopping to butter it she went back to the table and sat down with her cup of hot tea. She had really done it this time.

There was no way on earth that Robert would ever agree to the lease now. "Dear heaven," she said aloud. "How am I ever going to explain this to Laura . . . and to Mr. Martindale?" She lifted a spoonful of the amber liquid and let it cool. They had counted on her to pull it off. Now. . . . She sighed. This wasn't going to be one of her better days. Maybe her mother had been right when she said that women were emotionally ill-equipped to handle the frustrations of the business world.

The thought occurred to her again as she backed the car out of the garage. No! Emphatically no! Her mother had been wrong to put all women into the same category. Nan loved her job as much as her mother had loved her home. But some women needed more than a home. Nan knew beyond a doubt that the time would come when she would want a family of her own, but for now it was vital that she make good on her own. She was doing well in her chosen field . . . and she loved what she was doing, except in the matter of Robert Easton's lodge!

Laura was in her office when Nan arrived ten minutes early. Nan had worn a soft yellow dress in open defiance to her black mood. Putting her purse and briefcase on the desk, she waved at Laura and, taking the proverbial bull by the horns, decided to get the scene over with. "About yesterday," Nan began. "I'm afraid I didn't do quite as well as we had hoped."

"I know. You didn't get the contract yet."

Nan looked at her curiously then shrugged. "You guessed. Yes, I suppose it wasn't difficult. You knew I would have called you last night if I had."

"Look, a few hours won't make any difference. But you'd better get on the phone. Easton's office has been calling you for the last twenty minutes."

Nan sat down. "Calling? What about?"

"Well, the contract, of course. They said it would be ready at one o'clock. They had several questions. Since I couldn't get you on the phone I went ahead and gave them all the information I could. I didn't think you'd care. They want you to call back to verify the appointment."

Nan smiled weakly. "No . . . no. I don't mind. I'll call right away."

Laura reached out to touch her hand. "God! For you to pull

off something like this is just short of incredible. You're going to go to the top in the real estate business. Listen, Nan, this means a lot to me. I want you to know that."

Nan nodded, unable to speak. She was going to see him again. Suddenly that fact meant more to her than anything else in the world.

It was only with extreme concentration that she was able to get through the rest of the morning without making a number of mistakes. An enthusiastic call to Craig Martindale's office gave him the information that she was well on the way to closing a deal and was scheduled to pick up the contract later. He told her that the wheels had been set in motion hours ago and that he, along with a few members of his staff, would be in Tahoe the following day.

Her hands were shaking when she put down the phone. It was still too much to believe. Why had Robert agreed to the lease? She knew instinctively that he had no intention of going along with it earlier in the day. Was it his way of making amends for having manhandled her in the car? Or was there a chance, however remote, that he wanted to see her again as much as she wanted to see him?

The thought brought the old familiar warmth to the pit of her stomach and she had to pretend concentration on a computer printout of homes for sale from the multiple listing service. Betty was sitting at her desk in the corner of the room. If she looked up she could see Betty's face and above all, Nan didn't want to get into a discussion of her date the previous night. Betty lived a free and easy lifestyle and loved to compare notes over a cup of coffee. And Nan knew she couldn't talk about Robert, not yet. Finally, it was time to leave for the Easton Annex. After a trip to the ladies' room to run a comb through her hair and touch up her lipstick, Nan went in to tell Laura that she was leaving.

By the time she had parked and found her way to the elevator, Nan had become more than a little apprehensive. How would he act toward her after the incident in his car? She wasn't even sure how *she* ought to act toward *him*. They seemed destined to have a traumatic evening whenever they went out together. She stepped forward as the elevator door opened on the ninth floor. One thing for sure, he probably would never ask her out again, even though the evening had been quite enjoyable up until he had taken her home. Robert Easton wasn't the kind of man who liked having things blow up in his face.

She forced a smile as Claudia Mansfield, Robert's secretary, came forward.

"Mrs. Hendr...that is, Ms. Gilliam. How nice to see you again. We've been expecting you. Won't you step this way, please?"

Nan followed her down the corridor to a different office this time. *So far so good*, she thought. *At least his secretary is friendly*. The woman showed her to a comfortable-looking chair next to the desk and Nan sat down. A few minutes later Nan heard a door open behind her and she steeled herself for the confrontation with Robert.

"Hello, Ms. Gilliam. I'm Jameson Clark of Clark, Stern and Liebowitz. Mr. Easton asked me to handle this matter for him."

Nan, trying to cover her surprise that it was not Robert, shifted uneasily. "You're referring to the rental agreement on the lodge?"

He looked mildly interested. "Yes. Was there something else?"

"No. I...I didn't realize there had been enough time to have the agreement drawn up."

"He called me late last night and I got onto it right away. I think you'll find everything in order. The papers will have to be signed in triplicate by your client, and, under the circumstances, witnessed and notarized." He flipped through several pages of typescript. "On page four, clause seven, I would like to call your attention to a particular stipulation involving you, Ms. Gilliam."

She straightened. "Me? But I don't understand."

"It's nothing to worry about. The contract requires that you be on the premises whenever filming, or shooting as I believe they call it, is going on in the lodge. Of course the Easton firm will supplement your salary while you are away from the realty office."

Nan was appalled. "Does that mean I am directly responsible for what goes on at the lodge?"

"Not actually. As I understand the situation, Mr. Easton

feels that your being there as our representative may forestall any excessive damage. It gives you the right to close the lodge at any given moment should, in your judgment, the tenant become overly careless."

"But I can't possibly imagine that my client would agree to such a clause. I must tell you, Mr. Clark, I have no experience whatsoever in moviemaking."

"I can't see that your lack of movie experience would have any bearing on the matter. As for your other point, either your client accepts our conditions or there is no contract."

She stared at the papers. "This figure you are quoting for rent . . . it's astronomical."

"Yes, isn't it?" He smiled. "But don't worry. They can write it off on taxes." He stood, and Nan took it as a signal that the meeting was over. She remained where she was sitting.

"I . . . I really would like to discuss that particular clause with Mr. Easton. It is inconceivable that he meant for me to be present during the shooting of the movie."

He stood, waiting patiently. "Mr. Easton left for New York on the red-eye flight . . . just moments after he called me last night. It will be a week or more before he is expected to return. If I might make a suggestion, Ms. Gilliam. . . . Present the contract to your client. I can almost vouch for the fact that he won't find another property as desirable as this."

She got up and shook the hand he held out to her. "I don't think I have a great deal of choice. Thank you, Mr. Clark, for your time. My client will be in town tomorrow. I'll get back to you as soon as I have an answer."

He walked her out to the secretary's desk where he turned her over to Claudia Mansfield, who escorted her to the elevator. Nan suppressed a grin. She felt as if she were being guided through the Pentagon.

When she got back to the office she brushed aside the praise from Laura, Betty, and Fred. "Don't count on it yet. With a contract like this one, the man would have to be crazy to sign."

Laura laughed. "So what's the problem? They have to be a little crazy to be in the movie business in the first place. You might as well give him a call and lay it on the line."

Fifteen exhausting minutes later, Nan put the receiver back in its cradle as Laura and Betty stood waiting on the other side

of the desk. She shook her head. "Well, it's done. He accepted
the conditions, but I still won't believe it until he's signed the
contract." Laura and Betty grabbed each other and jumped up
and down in excitement until Betty nearly fell over Nan's desk.

"Good gosh. Have you figured out what your commission
will be?"

Nan laughed. "Not yet. I'm still trying to decide just what
it is they expect from me. I don't know a thing about the
movies."

Laura grinned. "Don't worry. I can fill you in on all the
background. It can't have changed all that much since I was
in front of the camera."

Betty looked at her with awe. "I didn't know you were an
actress. Do you know anybody famous?"

"Of course she does," Nan said, trying to cover Laura's
obvious embarrassment. "She even knows Craig Martindale,
the producer, and my client, no less."

"Hey, no kidding? Gee." Betty smiled dreamily. "I always
wanted to be in the movies. Maybe you could introduce me."

Laura gave her a playful shove. "Better stick to real estate,
Betty. It's a lot more fun than starving."

Betty made a face and went back to her desk.

When the office quieted down, Nan began making a list of
things she had to do as soon as Craig Martindale arrived. After
that she called Jameson Clark, Robert's attorney, to let him
know she had a tentative agreement on the contract.

"There is one stipulation, though," she said. "My client
would like to see the lodge before he signs the contract. I
assume his attorney will also want to look over the papers."

"Yes, of course. Suppose I send a key over by messenger
this afternoon? Of course, if your client fails to sign I will expect
immediate return of the key along with the contract."

As she hung up the phone, Nan shook her head in disbelief.
"A messenger, yet." She had expected, at the very least, to
have to drive over to pick up the key. They were certainly
giving her preferred-customer treatment. But why? She couldn't
figure it out. The only explanation she could see was that
Robert wanted to make up to her for past indignities. But why
then did he rush off to New York in the middle of the night?
Of course it could have been a business emergency, but some-

how she doubted that. She wanted to see him again if only to
convince herself that the feelings he had generated in her were
the product of a romantic setting and not an emotional involvement. Maybe seeing him in the light of day would accomplish
that, but from what the attorney had said, it would be nearly
a week before Robert would return.

Craig Martindale, having just checked into his hotel, called
the next morning minutes after Nan arrived at work. "Listen
honey, I hope you saved some time for me because I've gotta
have a look at the place this morning. You had breakfast or
do you wanna join me here for a cup of coffee?"

"Thank you. I've had breakfast but as soon as you are ready
to go up to the lodge, I'm available. The papers are all in order
for you to sign if you decide to go ahead with the deal."

"Terrific. I'll pick you up in the limo about ten."

Nan was ready and waiting when the limousine arrived,
accompanied by a pair of midnight-blue Lincoln Continentals.
She had worn a pale blue silk shirtwaist dress with a matching
blue sweater. A double-strand necklace of red beads matched
her red sandals and red shoulder bag which doubled as a briefcase.

The moment the blond man walked in the door of the realty
office she would have known him even if Betty hadn't seen
the entourage drive into the parking lot. She rose and went to
greet him.

"Mr. Martindale? I'm Nan Gilliam." She held out her hand
but he reached for both of them and spread her arms wide as
he surveyed her from head to foot.

"Well, well. You look even better than Foster Landon led
me to believe. And I thought L.A. had all the good-looking
broads."

Nan winced. "I'd like you to meet my boss . . ." She turned
toward Laura's office but it was empty. Betty hopped up from
her desk.

"Laura left just a few minutes ago." She smiled up at Craig
Martindale and batted her eyelashes.

Nan grinned despite herself. "Mr. Martindale, I'd like you
to meet my co-worker, Betty Lemmer."

He reached for Betty's hand and pressed it to his lips.

"Delighted, Betty . . . that is, if you will forgive my calling you by your first name."

Betty turned pink and smiled her gratitude. "Oh, that's fine, Mr. Martindale, just fine." It occurred to Nan that Craig Martindale had taken just the right approach with Betty. He obviously had charm to spare and knew how to use it.

Nan reached for her shoulder bag. "If you are ready, Mr. Martindale? . . ." He half bowed and motioned her to precede him.

"We'll ride in the limo," he said. "The rest of the group will follow in the other cars. If you've got the papers with you I'll give them to my lawyer to read on the way up there."

Nan took them out of her bag and handed them to him. While he walked over to the first Continental to talk to the attorney, she had a chance to study Craig Martindale. He was an extremely attractive man, probably in his early forties, trim, of medium height. He wore brown checked slacks topped off with a chocolate brown silk shirt which was laced at the front instead of buttoned. In the popular style, it was open halfway to his chest, a fad which Nan thought should be reserved only for men who boasted a more substantial growth of chest hair. A tan blazer was slung over his shoulder in the best television-commercial attitude of studied carelessness.

But his most outstanding feature was the wealth of thick blond hair which swept back from his high forehead in deep, shining waves. He had a habit of reaching up to pat it, much as a woman would a new hair-do, but oddly, the gesture was in no way effeminate. Craig Martindale exuded masculine appeal as consciously as if he were the star of his movies instead of the producer and director.

The chauffeur held the door of the limousine for her, then waited for Mr. Martindale. After a short delay he joined her and suggested that she give the chauffeur directions.

During the ride up the mountain Nan told him the general layout of the lodge and tried to get a feeling for what they would be doing.

"Mr. Martindale, I will certainly try to stay out of your way, but I'm afraid that I'll have to be at the site whenever filming is taking place. By the way, what kind of movie is it?"

Nan was intrigued by the animation that lit up his face as he hesitated for a minute. "It's called *Evil Heritage*, a story about a man who inherits a map from his father who had stolen it from another man and buried him alive in the desert. Most of it takes place in the Mojave, but some of the beginning and some of the final scenes will be shot here. It's a thriller..." He grinned. "Or at least that's what we intend it to be."

Nan leaned forward as they approached the turnoff into the Easton property. "Make a left up ahead where the gatepost marks the entrance. The lodge is a few hundred yards down the lane."

Craig Martindale swore softly. "This is gonna be a bitch of a place to get the sound trucks through."

"This is the narrowest part. The lane widens into a large parking area at the end."

If he was concerned about the obstacles to the approach, the first impression of the lodge itself appeared to have erased any doubts he might have had. He leaped out of the car, dragging Nan along with him.

"Judas! What a place. You couldn't have done better if you had been inside my head. It's exactly what I'm looking for."

"Wait until you see the interior. It's just fabulous." Nan unlocked the front door and motioned him inside.

He stood for a minute with his hands on his hips, then turned and swept Nan into his arms. Before she knew what was happening he had kissed her on both cheeks.

"Listen, honey. I'm taking you to dinner tonight. I heard about a spot that has terrific food, everything."

Nan laughed shakily as he put her down. She was not the type to hug and kiss people at random and it embarrassed her. "That's not necessary, Mr. Martindale. It was all part of the job."

"Look, honey. Forget the Mister business. My name's Craig. I'll call you Nan. Okay?" She nodded as he continued. "I'll send the car around for you at eight. Don't forget to give William your address."

"Thank you, but I don't think..."

"Let me do the thinking. I need someone to show me the town and I can't think of anyone more decorative than you."

He looked her up and down. "Wear something long and sexy."

Nan ran her tongue across her lips. *I'm not ready for this. In fact I might never be ready for it*, she thought, but she nodded. "All right. Eight it is."

Chapter Five

HE STILL HAD his arm around her when the rest of the entourage came in the front door. Nan took the opportunity to step away from him without making it too obvious. She could have saved the effort. He grabbed her around the waist and led her over to where the group of six or so people stopped to admire the room.

One woman stood out from the rest. A beautiful woman in her early thirties, with an abundance of silky dark hair, she was not concerned with the lodge or its furnishings. Instead, she fastened her gaze on Craig's arm where it circled Nan's waist. Craig held onto Nan with a proprietary air as he introduced her to the people who stood nearby.

"Didn't I tell you she'd do it? This is our girl, Nan Gilliam. Nan, meet Dwight Huddleston, my lawyer. This is Stan Cooperston, my locations coordinator, and this is Cassie Rinella, my assistant." The coordinator was a bald-headed man, tall

and competent looking. Nan recognized the warning signals
Cassie Rinella was broadcasting. It wasn't hard to guess that
she had her sights set for Craig.

It was the lawyer, a dark-haired man whom Nan thought
of as having the manicured look, who spoke first. "Listen
Craig, I've looked at the contract. It's a killer. You'd be a fool
to sign it. They'll have your hands tied no matter which way
you turn."

Craig Martindale's voice was deceptively soft. "We're between the rock and the hard place, Dwight. If we don't start
shooting next week it'll cost us more than we'd save by not
signing."

"I still think we should have shot the scenes on the lot."

"You know the backers wouldn't buy that. Besides," he
grinned as he spoke, "we can write it off come tax time. Why
do ya think I picked Tahoe for location? I've been itching to
get in a few days at the casinos." As if dismissing the attorney,
he turned to the coordinator. "Whaddaya think, Stan? Can we
get the lights and equipment set up in here without spending
a fortune?"

"We'll have to have some lines run up here, but logistics-
wise, we're in good shape. With these high ceilings we
shouldn't have any real problems getting the dollies and the
crane in. There's plenty of room to move around."

Nan creased her forehead. "What about the floors? Won't
the heavy equipment ruin them?"

Stan shook his head. "We'll cover the floors with fiber
padding. Not just for your sake, but to keep it soundproof when
the cameras start rolling around."

Cassie went over to Craig Martindale and linked her arm
through his. "I'm just dying to see the casinos. Sammy Davis
is the headliner at the Sahara. Are you going to take me tonight?"

"Not tonight, sweetie. You need your beauty sleep. Maybe
tomorrow night." Cassie pulled a strand of her long dark hair
across her mouth, testing it with her lips. She didn't respond
to his rebuff, but the look she gave Nan was less than friendly.

They took a quick tour of the remainder of the house, checking out the large kitchen and dining room which would be used
briefly in the filming of the movie. When Craig saw the hot-

tub room with the trout stream running through, he got excited
and began snapping his fingers.

"Listen, Cassie. Get on the phone when we get back to the
hotel and tell the writers to come up with a hot-tub scene.
Maybe they can fit it in right before the car chase down the
mountain."

"Georgie isn't going to like it."

"He will when he sees the layout. It's a natural. Just do it,
will ya?"

She shrugged and made a notation on her small note pad.
An hour later they had seen all they wanted to see and had
returned to town.

Laura's car was in the drive when they pulled into the
parking lot at Pinnacle Realty. Nan reached for her handbag
containing the contract which the lawyer had returned to her.

"If you'll come inside we can have the contracts witnessed,
signed, and notarized. I'd really like to have you meet my
boss."

He got out and held the door for her then walked over to
the lead Continental and apparently told them they could go
on to the hotel. Once inside, Nan tapped on the door to Laura's
office but there was no response. She looked over at Betty who
shrugged.

"Don't ask me. Laura was here not five minutes ago. She
must've gone out the other door."

Her absence really didn't matter because Fred Erdman and
Betty witnessed and notarized the contracts after Craig signed
them, but Nan was puzzled over Laura's behavior.

Despite Nan's hopes that Craig would forget his promise
to take her out to dinner, he had reminded her about it just
before he left the office. As the time grew closer to eight
o'clock she began to get a little nervous. She didn't need this.
The contract was already signed and delivered to Robert
Easton's attorney. Why did she have to go out to dinner with
Craig Martindale? She laughed. No doubt half the women in
Hollywood would give their right arm for a date with Craig,
yet she would have been happy to spend the evening at home
alone. The casino scene had never held any great attraction for
her.

She slipped the navy blue sheath over her head and settled the floor-length skirt around her hips. "Well, Mr. Craig Martindale, it's not exactly sexy," she said to herself, "but it's the best I can do." She fastened a double strand of tiny cultured pearls around her neck, pearls which her father had given to her mother on their twenty-fifth wedding anniversary. Seeing them against her throat brought quick tears to Nan's eyes. No, she couldn't allow herself to think about her mother. There was too much sadness, too much bitterness there. Would she never get over that feeling of loss, she wondered? If her mother had died suddenly the way her father had when his car went out of control it would have been different. But to die because a group of greedy promoters...

She was almost grateful to hear the doorbell. It never accomplished anything to dredge up the old hurts surrounding her mother's death at the nursing home.

Craig Martindale greeted her with a hug and a kiss on each cheek. She schooled herself not to draw away even though such easy shows of affection were distasteful to her.

"You look terrific, honey. I had Cassie make reservations at the King Midas. They say it's got the best of everything. I hear there's a great floor show. Sound okay?"

Nan nodded with what she hoped passed for enthusiasm. Inwardly she was hoping that they would have a table near the back. The Golden Slipper Club at the King Midas Hotel was the club where Lance was master of ceremonies, and one thing for sure—she was in no mood to see him tonight.

Nan discovered that, despite her reservations, being with Craig was a trip! She had never experienced anything like it in her life. Even her date with Robert, well-known as he was, was nothing compared to the stir Craig Martindale created when he walked into the casino lobby of the hotel. It was probably the differences in their personalities. Where Robert was cool and dignified in his bearing, causing people to stand in awe of him, Craig was the charmer, Mr. Show Business himself. People flocked around him and he seemed to thrive on it. He also gloried in showing off Nan as if she were a newly acquired possession, and the attention put her in high spirits.

She managed reasonably well until they entered the dining

room of the Golden Slipper Club and were met by the maître
d'. He bowed effusively as he assured Craig Martindale how
honored the staff of the King Midas was to have him as their
guest. As Nan feared, he directed them to a table front and
center. This club had none of the intimacy of the smaller ones.
People went to the Golden Slipper to see and be seen. Large,
crescent-shaped booths were placed in tiers to give those seated
toward the rear a clear view of the stage.

Nan avoided looking up as she slid into the ultracomfortable
seat. Fortunately the maître d' blocked her view of the stage
for the time, but she knew that Lance was due to appear in a
few minutes and she dreaded what he might say. He was so
unpredictable, so uninhibited when he had a chance to put
someone on the hot spot.

They were just finishing their appetizer of shrimp tempura
when a drum roll began and attention was drawn to center stage
where Lance stood behind the floor mike, his hand upraised
for quiet.

"Ladies and gentlemen, it is with great honor that the Golden
Slipper Club of the King Midas Hotel introduces a visiting
V.I.P. from Hollywood. With us tonight is the eminent producer, director, and man of many talents, Mr. Craig Martindale."

The spotlights split and a beam of bright light flooded the
booth where Nan and Craig were sitting. She would like to
have gone under the table but he took it as if it were homage
due him. He half rose in his seat, inclined his head in a slight
nod, and smiled broadly.

Lance continued. "The word is out that Mr. Martindale is
in town with a crew from Regal Studios to begin filming his
latest thriller, *Evil Heritage.*" He did a double-take as he saw
Nan seated next to Craig. "And seated next to him, looking
even more lovely than usual, is Tahoe's newest real estate
tycoon, Nan Hendricks." He turned to the bandleader who
signaled for another roll of the drums. "Let's dedicate the next
song to them, maestro."

Nan's face felt as if it were burning and she prayed that it
didn't show in the spotlight. Craig turned to her. "So, my dear,
you are a celebrity in your own right. I can't say I'm surprised.

With your face and figure you should make it big." His voice lost some of its charm. "But what's this Hendricks jazz? I thought your name was Gilliam."

"It is. I was married once and after the divorce went through I went back to using my maiden name."

"Hendricks, Hendricks." He snapped his fingers. "I just heard that name tonight."

She sighed. "Lance Hendricks, the emcee, was my husband."

He nodded. "How long since your divorce?"

"Three months, a little over."

"Rough. The first year is the hardest they say. Me, I've never taken the plunge. You makin' it all right?"

She shrugged. "I manage." The last thing she wanted was a discussion of her marital state or lack of it . . . particularly with a stranger. She was grateful when the waiter brought their dinner and the attention of the audience returned to the comedian on stage.

It became apparent after they finished their dinner that Craig Martindale was telling the truth when he said the main reason he wanted to shoot part of the film in Tahoe was so that he could gamble. They walked into the casino and he signaled to a change girl to give them a stack of quarters. He handed Nan a paper cup full to the brim. "Here, honey. Let's see how you make out with the slots."

She shook her head. "I'd really rather not. You go ahead. I'll watch over your shoulder."

He shrugged and picked a machine. The woman next to him was seated on a stool in front of four slot machines. She glared at Craig. "You can use the end one but these are mine," she told him. Before he could answer she grabbed three coins and put them into the machine in front of her. Reaching for the handle with her gloved right hand, she gave it a mighty yank. It came up a cherry, lemon, and bar. She swore competently and repeated the process with the other three machines. A few minutes later the first machine had paid off a dollar and the third machine had spit out over five dollars in quarters. The women let them accumulate in the pan and fed another stack of coins into the machine. Nan was dying to ask her how long she had been sitting there, but it was obvious the woman didn't want to take time away from her gambling just to talk. If the condition of her glove was any indication, she must have been at the machine for days.

Craig wasn't doing as well. He had dropped about ten dollars into the machine when he looked up in disgust. "This is a sucker's game. Pick me another machine, honey."

"I don't know anything about the slot machines. They all operate in the house's favor." He gave her a look and she shrugged. "All right. How about the one in the corner? No one is using it."

He walked over and dropped four quarters into the machine called Big Red. Almost before the handle was down a small handful of quarters rained into the slot with a metallic clatter. Craig let out a whoop in boyish delight as he scooped them out and put them in his paper cup. The next pull brought him a dollar. Three pulls later he hit the two-hundred-dollar jackpot, lighting up the flasher on top of the machine and ringing a raucous alarm bell. If he had expected a crowd to assemble he was disappointed. A few people paused in their gambling long enough to look up and reveal the envy on their faces but the only one to approach was the bored-looking change girl in her short-skirted uniform. She paid him off and reminded him to take off the winner. He obligingly put another quarter into the slot. As he did, five more quarters dropped into the pan.

He turned to Nan and grinned. "Listen, honey, you've got good instincts. Remind me not to forget that."

She yawned and laughed. "My instincts, good or not, tell me this would be a good time to call it a night. You're way ahead. Wouldn't that be a nice way to leave it? Besides I have to work tomorrow and it is rather late."

He looked at his watch. "I was going to try a hand of blackjack, but I'll tell you what. Give me two more pulls and then I'll take you home. Okay?"

She laughed. "Sure."

His next two pulls came up dry and he looked at her pleadingly. She returned his look but didn't say anything. "Okay, have it your way. You're determined that I go home a winner, aren't you?"

"I can't think of a better way to end a day."

He stared at her speculatively. "Neither can I, honey, neither can I."

It was only later, in the limousine, that Nan knew what he had been thinking. As they got into the car, he casually put his arm around the back of the seat and let it lie there without touching her. Nan was aware of what he had in mind. She was also extremely conscious of the chauffeur, even though a glass partition was raised between the front and rear seats of the car and he was careful to keep his gaze straight in front of him.

Craig reached up and coiled a strand of her hair around his finger. "That was fun, but I haven't gone home this early since I was in high school. Why don't we go someplace for a nightcap?"

"Thank you, but no."

His hand dropped to her shoulder and he turned her toward him. "You could invite me in."

Nan looked at the chauffeur and edged away. Craig grinned. "You don't have to worry about William. He's blind."

Nan missed the joke until Craig started to laugh. "Well, in a manner of speaking. He never sees what goes on in the back seat."

They pulled into her drive and William discreetly turned off the motor and sat facing forward. Nan felt her palms begin to perspire. "I really must go in, Craig. Thank you for dinner. It was lovely." As she reached for the door handle he took his arm away and sighed.

"Hold it. You're the boss. Next time I'll drive the Continental."

He saw her to the door and, taking her key, unlocked it for her. She turned toward him, effectively blocking the door. "Thank you again, Craig."

He reached for her shoulders and, bending down, kissed her chastely on the mouth. A moment later he turned to leave. "Tomorrow night," he yelled over his shoulder, "I'm taking you to the Sahara."

Later, as she was getting ready for bed, Nan laughed at his nerve. Maybe that was the way they did things in Hollywood...or maybe he just assumed she was flattered by his attention. Whether she wanted to go out with him again she still hadn't decided. Laura and Betty kept telling her that it was time she started seeing men again, but her divorce was still too new for her to be completely at ease where most men were concerned. On the other hand she had to admit that it was like entering a new world when she walked into a casino or supper club on the arm of Craig Martindale. The service was considerably better, the smiles were brighter, and everyone seemed to be eager to please. She had never thought it was important to go first class, but she knew that first class meant more than the obvious luxuries—it was a state of mind. When people treated you as if you were special, you felt special.

She laughed at herself. Craig Martindale certainly wasn't the type of man to whom she was attracted, but he was interesting and he would only be here for a short time.

He took her to dinner the next two nights, followed always by a turn at the gambling tables, either blackjack or baccarat. Nan had seen the baccarat room with its glass partitions which separated it from the rest of the casino, and its three dealers dressed in dark tuxedos with elegantly ruffled white shirts, but she had never been inside the room. It was here that the elite—the gentlemen in evening dress and the ladies with gowns cut to the waistline in back—spent their gambling money. Next to the High Rollers room, which most casinos had on a private floor, the baccarat room was the most prestigious in the casino. She stood behind Craig while he played. The sounds were muted here. That in itself was worth something, but she no longer seemed to bring him luck and he soon moved on to try his hand at the roulette wheel.

On the third night they were just leaving the slot machines when Nan saw Lance at the craps table. He noticed her at the same time and waved a greeting but was so involved with his game that he immediately looked away. Nan felt sick inside. He had changed rapidly, and for the worse, since their divorce. If ever she questioned the rightness of her decision to put an end to their marriage, seeing him like this negated those questions.

Craig put his hand over hers. "What say we have a few drinks in the lounge? Maybe my luck will change."

"What I'd really like is something to eat and a cup of coffee.

Does that sound all right?"

"A poor substitute." He grinned. "But at least you didn't insist on going home. I can get some booze in the dining room."

They were ushered to a table in the center of the room but Craig refused it and pointed to a secluded corner table. Nan wasn't as hungry as she had pretended and when her club sandwich came she merely toyed with it. The waitress kept Craig supplied with drinks and as the abundantly endowed girl bent over the table, it occurred to Nan that liquor wasn't all she was selling.

Craig was becoming more difficult to handle. Nan finally reached for her bag. "It's time to go, Craig. Will you please let me drive tonight?"

"F'get it, honey. I'm not drunk. I never drink much any-more. Besides, I c'n still drive better than you even when I'm s-seeing double." He threw a wad of bills on the table and would have left them but Nan saw that three of them were hundreds.

"Craig, I think you'd better sit down again. You can't leave that much money. There must be five hundred dollars or more in that stack of bills." Reaching across the table, she peeled off several of the bills and shoved them into his breast pocket.

He grabbed her roughly by the arm and pulled her against him. "Honey, you sh-sure take good c-care of me. Come on, gimme a big kiss then let's go home and s-spend the night at your house."

She tried to push him away, but, intoxicated as he was, his grip bit into her arm. "Behave yourself, Craig. You're making us look ridiculous."

"Who c-cares? Maybe we'll give them a thrill." His laugh carried across the room and people were beginning to stare. He refused to let go of her arm and instead planted a huge, sloppy kiss on her cheek. "Loosen up, lady. After all, you're supposed to be a liberated woman."

"That's enough, Craig. Give me the keys to the Continental. I'm going to drive you back to the hotel."

"Not on your life, honey. I'm the man. I d-do the driving."

Nan was beginning to fume. She motioned to a waiter. "Would you please call the desk clerk at Harrah's and ask them to send Mr. Martindale's limousine here at once?"

"Yes, ma'am. Right away."

He was back in a few minutes with a pleased look on his face. "Mr. Martindale's chauffeur is on his way. Is there anything I can do?"

"I don't think so, thank you."

Craig stared at her for a moment, his eyes flat and glassy. "You trying to ditch me, lady?"

"No, Craig. I'm just trying to get you home in one piece. Can you walk out to the lobby?"

"S-stayin' here and so are you."

"I'm leaving right now, whether you are or not."

He took hold of her wrist, grasping it tightly between his fingers. "Nobody w-walks out on m-me."

Nan felt tears of pain begin to sting her eyelids and she bit her lip to keep from crying out.

A shadow fell across the table. "Let go of her arm, Mr. Martindale. You're hurting the lady."

She would have known that voice anywhere. As she looked up into his eyes, she flushed with surprise. It wasn't so much that he had been witness to her embarrassment that bothered her, it was the fact that she was so glad to see him that appalled her. His dark hair fell across his forehead and he brushed it away as he put his hand on Craig's shoulder in an authoritative gesture.

Robert glanced at her for a moment without speaking, then sat down next to Craig. Looking at the two men, Nan drew a deep breath and thought to herself, *So what happens now? This is getting to be a very tricky situation.*

Chapter Six

CRAIG GAVE HIM a contemptuous look. "Wh-who the devil d'you think you are?"

"I'm Robert Easton. My company owns this hotel and casino. You're creating a disturbance, Mr. Martindale, and I'd like to make sure that you return safely to your hotel. We value our customers and don't like to see them get hurt."

"In a pig's eye."

Nan rubbed her wrist in an attempt to restore circulation. "It's all right, Robert. I can manage. I've sent for his limousine. He won't let me drive and he could never make it on his own."

Robert nodded. "I assume you came here with him. I'll see that you get home. You certainly can't ride with him in his condition."

Nan wasn't about to argue with his last statement, but she wasn't sure that she wanted to ride with Robert. The last time she had been alone in a car with him she'd had to walk home. She couldn't meet his gaze.

"No . . . thanks anyway, but I'll just call a cab."

"Don't be childish." He looked toward the entrance of the restaurant. "Would that be his chauffeur?"

"Yes. That's William." She put her hand under Craig's arm. "Come on now. William's here with the car."

Surprisingly, he stood up without complaint and let Nan and Robert guide him to the door where William took over for her. She smiled. "Thank you for coming so quickly, William. Mr. Martindale has had a little too much to drink and would like to go back to the hotel."

They helped him out to the limousine which was parked under the overhead. Nan motioned toward the parking lot. "The Continental is parked in G section. He wouldn't give me the keys so I guess someone will have to pick it up later."

"May I drop you off at your house, Miss Gilliam?"

Before she could answer, Robert took her arm. "Miss Gilliam and I are old friends. I'll see that she gets home safely."

William touched two fingers to his cap then went around the car and got in. Craig had fallen over on the seat, probably passed out, Nan thought. She would have been perfectly safe with him and she told Robert so.

He gave her a look that left no doubt as to his feelings but it did little to make her less uncomfortable. For all she knew she was going from the frying pan into the fire. He took her inside and told her to sit down while he went to the desk and spoke to the hostess. A short time later the doorman signaled that the car had been brought around.

Robert reached for her hand. "Shall we?" he asked as he motioned toward the car.

She got up reluctantly. The comfortable warmth of his hand sent tingles of anticipation through her. Whether consciously or unconsciously he was rubbing the back of her hand with his thumb. It was like a lover's caress, the suggestion so intense that it sent heat flooding through her body. She pulled away and he appeared not to notice as he opened the limousine door and motioned for her to get in.

Before she knew what had happened, he had said goodnight and closed the door after her.

"Where to, Miss Gilliam?" the driver asked.

She stammered slightly and gave him her address.

The traffic was unusually heavy as he made his way down
Route 50 on the Nevada side of the lake. She was glad that
driving required enough of his attention to prevent him from
noticing her obvious irritation. This was too much. It was just
inconceivable that Robert had stayed behind while his driver
took her home in the limousine. Did he find her so unattrac-
tive and so uninteresting that he was bored with her company?
The least he could have done was to stay around long enough
to give her time to thank him for leasing the lodge to the movie
company.

She shifted in the seat, uncomfortable with her mixed
emotions. On one hand she was frightened of being alone with
him. He affected her more deeply than she wanted to admit.
But in another sense, she had been so long without the comfort
of a man's arms around her that her body ached to have him
hold her.

After they crossed Stateline the traffic finally cleared enough
that they were able to move freely until it picked up again at
the intersection of Lake Tahoe Boulevard and Emerald Bay
Road. Once they passed the entrance to Camp Richardson they
had a clear track all the way to Rubicon Bay.

As the limousine slowed for the turn into her street, Nan
leaned forward. A car was parked in her driveway. There was
no mistaking that sleek, silver-gray Maserati. It was Robert's.
But what was he doing here? She had just left him less than
a half-hour ago at the Golden Slipper Club.

The chauffeur pulled in behind the car and stopped, then
got out and held the door for Nan. If he was curious about the
car being there, he was too well trained to let it show. Nan
nodded in his direction. "Goodnight, Arthur. Thank you."

"You're quite welcome, Miss Gilliam. Goodnight."

She waited until he had left before she went over to the car.
Robert got out as she approached and stood alongside, resting
his hand on the shiny top. Nan was confused by his being there
and the confusion changed to irritation at his silence.

"What are you doing here? I thought we said goodnight
back at the Golden Slipper."

"I changed my mind." He motioned toward the front door.
"Will you invite me in?"

She thought about it for a moment. "I don't know, Robert. It's pretty late."

"But you're not Cinderella and I'm not Prince Charming. So what's the problem?"

She laughed. "You've got a point there."

He took the key and unlocked the door then waited for her to turn on the light. Going into the living room she switched on two table lamps and a floor lamp.

"Sit down, if you like. I want to hang up my wrap."

"If you had warned me that you like so much light I'd have brought my sunglasses," he said.

Her face turned pink. "I'm sorry. I thought . . . well, I guess three are a little much." She reached over and turned off the floor lamp, then took a chair opposite him. He looked completely relaxed with his arm across the back of the sofa.

"I came to apologize to you for the other night . . . and for what happened all those years ago. I never intended you to find out . . . not that that makes it less inexcusable. But you have to believe this. . . . When I picked you up at your house that night I was *glad* that I had asked you to the dance. And I was proud of the way you handled the situation. You had courage and I admired you for it." He ran his hands through his hair. "I should have told you that night but I was ashamed and embarrassed at having been found out. And as for the other night, I guess I simply wanted an excuse to kiss you. I hope you'll forgive me. I'm not in the habit of manhandling ladies."

Nan drew her finger along the welting on the arm of the chair. "You don't have to apologize. Your signing of the rental agreement was apology enough. I know that you really didn't want to lease the lodge to the movie company, and I can't tell you how much it means to me that you agreed."

He grinned. "Come on now. How could I pass up a chance to have my roof repaired for free?"

Her blush deepened. "I think we've exhausted the subject. Could I get you something to drink?"

"What I'd really like is something to eat. I noticed you hadn't touched your sandwich back at the club. Are you hungry?"

Nan suddenly realized she was starved. "I'm famished. Why

don't we go out to the kitchen and see what's in the refrigerator?"

"I was going to suggest we go to the Sahara or the Nugget."

She lifted her eyebrows. "Afraid of my cooking?"

"I'll try anything once. Just lead the way."

The kitchen was where most people congregated when they visited the Gilliam house. It was a large family-type kitchen divided from the breakfast room by a counter which was equipped with barstools. Robert straddled one.

"Will you let me help?"

"Not only let...I insist on it. Do you like steak? I just happen to have a nice porterhouse that I bought yesterday and haven't had a chance to put in the freezer."

"Great." He raised an eyebrow. "Medium rare?"

"Is there another way? How about a salad? I have some romaine and red cabbage."

He grinned. "Is this where I'm supposed to step up and volunteer to make the dressing?"

"Is that an offer?"

"I make the worst dressing in the world, but if you have a loaf of unsliced bread and some garlic, I'll make some garlic bread that's just short of outrageous. I'll also take over the coffee concession if you like."

"Wonderful." She motioned to the pantry. "There's almost a full loaf of sourdough bread in the bread box and you'll find some garlic buds in a jar on the second shelf. I don't have a press so you'll have to do it the hard way. The butter's in the refrigerator."

While she waited for the gas grill on the deck to heat up, she set the table with quilted orange place mats and yellow and white plates and mugs. A bouquet of orange nasturtiums in a white wicker basket matched the white linen napkins with the nasturtium flowers appliqued in the corners. After that she made the salad and when it was finished the steak was almost ready.

Robert toasted the bread under the broiler in the oven, bringing it still sizzling to the table just as Nan carried in the platter with the steak.

"I hope you're very hungry," she said. "This steak's bigger than I thought it was."

"Just watch me." He held her chair and when she was seated, sat down across from her. "We ought to go into the restaurant business together. We make a great team."

She laughed. "One meal does not a restaurant make. I'm really not a great cook. Anyone can broil a steak, but your garlic bread and the coffee are fabulous."

"Next time I'll broil a lobster for us. Now that will be unforgettable."

Nan realized that she was happier than she had been in months. It was fun to cook for a man, especially when they did it together. And he was already talking about the next time. She tried hard not to let herself believe there was a future for them, but she wanted so much for it to happen.

They sat for a while over their coffee talking about local problems, the expansion and growth of the Tahoe community, pollution of the lake, the deep water probe and its abortive end. But below their casual conversation ran an undercurrent of emotion. Nan felt it. She wondered if Robert also sensed what was happening between them.

After they finished eating they carried their plates to the sink where Nan stacked them. "Uh-uh," she said as he started to rinse them. "I let my guests cook but I don't let them do the dishes. After you leave I'll put them in the dishwasher."

"That isn't a subtle hint, is it?"

"No. If I wanted you to go, I'd ask you to leave."

He focused his gaze on her face. "Thank you. I'll file that away for future reference."

Nan felt a little embarrassed by her own candor and fumbled with the tie of the big apron which had protected her evening gown. Instead of untying it she only succeeded in making a knot.

He stepped behind her. "May I?"

She nodded. He struggled with it for several seconds then swore softly under his breath.

"Remind me not to let you touch the lines on my boat." He bent closer and she felt his warm breath flutter the hair at the base of her neck. It was disconcerting. She wished he would hurry.

"Just break it if you have to," she said in desperation. "I can sew it back together."

"Don't rush me. I like to do things slow and easy."

"Sorry."

"'S okay. There. I told you I'd do it." He untied the apron from around her waist and for a moment his arms encircled her. It was all she could do to keep from swaying into them but she didn't recognize his touch as an invitation.

Slow and easy, is it? she thought. *Then you have more will-power than I do.* She moved away quickly in the hope that he didn't suspect her feelings. "Would you like to watch television?" she asked.

"No. Would you?"

She was relieved. It would have been impossible to sit calmly next to him as he watched a television program. "No. Not particularly."

"What *would* you like to do?"

She stared at him. *Is he putting me on?* "I . . . it's rather late."

"Are you asking me to leave this time?"

She shook her head.

"I'm grateful for that, because I really don't want to go." He hesitated. "Could we walk down to the lake?"

She breathed a sigh of relief. "Yes, if you like. I'll just get a sweater."

She flipped a switch which lighted the area near the house but gave almost no illumination down by the lake. "The path is easy until you get down to the beach, then the sand is pretty soft."

He looked down at her. "You'll get sand in your shoes."

She laughed. "Maybe that's why they call them sandals. It doesn't matter. The sand brushes off."

"This can't be much fun for you. Would you have rather gone to the casino?"

She looked up at him in surprise. "Not at all. Would you?"

He shook his head. "I never gamble for pleasure. Actually, I have very little to do with the casinos. Another part of the company manages that angle. I'm more into development and construction. Fortunately, the casinos operate very well in spite of, or more probably because of, the fact I let the other division handle them."

She leaned against an oak tree and looked out over the

water. "It's so beautiful, isn't it . . . our Lake Tahoe?"

"The most perfect spot on earth. Where else can you find crystal clear water hundreds of feet deep with a backdrop of snow-capped mountains several months of the year? Just breathe that air. It's even better out on the water."

"If it were daylight I'd take you out in the boat."

He looked at her in surprise. "You have a boat?"

"Of course. It's tied up at the end of the pier."

He shaded his eyes against the moonlight. "I can't see it in the dark."

"Come on. I'll show you." She took his hand and led him up the steps and onto the long, wooden dock. "See, there it is."

He walked over and stood against the railing. "Are you talking about the rowboat?"

"Of course. What did you think?"

He threw his head back and laughed. "You'd never believe what I was thinking. Can you handle it by yourself?"

"Certainly. We even have a ten-horse motor I put on when I want to go any distance."

"We? Your former husband and you?"

She flushed and was glad he couldn't see her face in the semidarkness. "No, not Lance. I was thinking of my parents. It's hard to think of them as dead."

She started to walk over to the railing, but the toe of her slipper caught on a loose board and she stumbled. He caught her and held her for a moment, then turned her in his arms until she was facing him.

"Nan. You are so beautiful." He pulled her against him and brushed his mouth against her lips, soft as a leaf drifting on the surface of the lake.

Nan was overcome by her need for him and yearned to let herself melt against him, but she held back. She had made one mistake with Lance when she let her heart rule her head. She couldn't afford to make another. She needed time, time to get her life together before she thought about getting involved with another man.

His mouth had traced a line of fire across her face and she clenched her fingers against her sides. At last he held her at arm's length and looked down at her.

"Is it me, or something I said?"

She shook her head, afraid to trust her voice.

"Look, I don't want to rush you. I just thought that I, that we..." He took a deep breath. "I thought that we had something going for us."

To save herself, she couldn't talk but stared up at him in mute agony.

He pulled her closer as if to gauge her expression. "You're still angry with me for the things I've done to you in the past. That's it, isn't it?"

"No. That's not it. I just..." She couldn't finish.

He let her go and stepped back. "I think maybe it's time we called it a night."

She nodded. Maybe it was better that way. Better to end it before it got to the point where it was out of control. He waited for her to precede him to the house, then followed close behind. Once inside he made straight for the front door. She followed. He turned to look back at her after he opened the door. Nan was sure he had planned to say something, but he sighed and said goodnight without waiting for a response.

She stood in the doorway for several minutes after his car had backed out of the drive. The sense of loss was almost unbearable. She wanted to give herself over to the luxury of tears but she had learned long ago that tears were at best a temporary cure. She had cried all her tears the night her mother had died in her room at the new rest home where she had been moved after the eviction from the old one.

Dear God, she thought. Why must I keep remembering it? It's over and there's nothing I can do about it now. But it was always so. Whenever something happened to make her sad she was forced to relive the times when her mother had pleaded with Nan not to let them move her. But progress had won out against justice in the court battle. The nursing home was forced to close down and move to new quarters. Three days after the move Nan's mother had died, still begging to be taken back to her old room. Nan had been with her at the time and she never forgot the fear on her mother's face.

Tears welled up against her lids and she brushed them away impatiently. It was foolish to cry over things she couldn't change. Slipping out of her gown, she pulled on a terrycloth robe and went into the kitchen to do the dishes. Robert's napkin, rumpled and unfolded where he had left it, lay on the counter. She picked it up, pleating it between her fingers. It had been a wonderful evening once she had put Craig into the limousine. Robert, for all his wealth and prestige, had seemed perfectly at home in her kitchen. Why couldn't she have been equally relaxed? She had wanted him to kiss her, he must have known that. Why couldn't she have let it happen? It wasn't as if he had planned to seduce her. She was convinced that he would have stopped at a single word from her.

She shoved the rack of dishes into the dishwasher and slammed the door. But that was the trouble. He would have been able to stop, but would she? She rinsed the sponge and drew it across the counter. That was one question it was safer not to answer. She wasn't even sure that she could.

It was only later when she got into bed that she realized she had carried his napkin with her and laid it on the nightstand. Punching her pillow into a neat mound, she picked up the napkin and held it against her lips as she reached up to turn off the light. There was the faint smell of garlic mingled with a whisper of aftershave lotion. The combination was pleasant and she lay back and closed her eyes as she stretched out full length. The king-size bed which she dearly loved had never seemed so empty. It occurred to her that her life was in a similar state. She had everything she needed to be comfortable but without someone to share it, the emptiness was overwhelming.

It was then that the phone rang. She sat up and turned on the light. "Hello."

"It's Robert. I have to talk to you, Nan."

Chapter Seven

HEARING NO RESPONSE, his voice, at first controlled, took on an uneasy tone. "Nan, are you there?"

She swallowed. "Yes... I'm here."

"Did I waken you?"

"No. I'm in..." She had started to say in bed but thought better of it. "I'm still awake. What is it, Robert? You sound a little strange. Are you all right?"

He laughed without humor. "In the sense you mean... yes. I couldn't sleep with the way things were between us when I left your house." There was a long silence, as if each were waiting for the other to speak.

"Why didn't you want me to kiss you, Nan?"

"I... I don't know."

"Like hell you don't. I'd like an honest answer. Or doesn't it mean anything to you that I'm hurting?"

"Of course it does. How can you say such a thing?"

"Look, I've been lying here in bed thinking about you and

it doesn't make sense unless you still haven't forgiven me. God knows I'm not heaven's gift to womanhood but I can't be that hard to take."

She laid down upon the pillow and cradled the phone against her shoulder. "Must we talk about it now?"

"Can you think of a better time? I'd like to see you again soon, but I've got to know where I stand. Did you fix dinner for me just because I agreed to lease the lodge? Were you just out to settle a debt?"

"That's the last thing I had in mind."

"Then what?"

She ran her tongue over her lips. "I don't know if I can make you understand, Robert. I . . . I haven't been lucky where men are concerned. I've been hurt too many times. My high-school days were an absolute nightmare. College was better but I never met anyone I cared enough about to allow them to hurt me." He made a sympathetic sound as she continued. "Then there was Lance. I thought I loved him, but he wanted a mother and I soon discovered it wasn't much fun playing parent to a grown man." She sighed. "It's going to take me a while to get over that. I couldn't stand to be hurt again . . . not yet."

His voice was husky with emotion. "God, Nan. I wish I were there with you. I want to hold you."

She looked at the rumpled sheets and felt a moment of panic. "No. You can't come over."

There was a pause, then he chuckled softly. "I didn't mean I planned to . . ." There was another pause. "Are you in bed?"

She considered lying then changed her mind. "Have you been drinking?"

"No. Drinking never made me feel like this. You have a very nice bed. I like the white tapestry bedspread."

She sat up straight. "I don't know what you mean."

He laughed boyishly. "The devil you don't. I looked in the door of your bedroom while you were turning the steaks. I have a king-size, too."

There was a long pause while she tried to catch her breath. She should never have told him how she felt. Now he must surely know that she was attracted to him. She chewed at her lower lip, then tried to make her voice sound cool. "Is there anything else you wanted to know in order to go to sleep?"

"Yes. Which side of the bed do you sleep on?"

She caught her breath. The very nerve of the man! He didn't deserve to know the truth. "If I tell you will you stop bothering me?"

"I certainly hope not, but I'll promise to hang up and let you go to sleep."

She looked down at the empty right side of the bed. "I sleep on the right side."

"Uh-oh. We've a problem. So do I."

"That settles it, then. There's no future for us."

"I'm willing to change."

"No, Robert. It would be asking too much to change a habit ingrained since childhood. I think we'd better forget the whole thing. I'm going to hang up now."

"I was right. You're still angry because of the way I treated you in the past."

Her voice reflected her impatience. "What must I do to convince you you're wrong?"

He laughed deep in his throat. "I thought you'd never ask." Nan tried to think of a sharp retort but he didn't give her time to answer. "You blushed, didn't you? Don't bother to protest. I know you better than you think I do. But getting back to your question. You can convince me by having dinner with me tomorrow night."

Nan was silent. If she agreed, she knew instinctively that her emotional attachment to him would pass the point of no return. But if she refused it would be the end. Robert Easton had his pride, too. She was not likely to be given another chance to change her mind. He was like no man she had ever met or would ever meet again. She had recognized the fact even during her high-school days. Could she afford to let him slip away without giving herself a chance? She blinked her eyes rapidly.

"What time will you pick me up?"

"How about right now?"

"Silly. I meant for dinner tomorrow night."

"As early as possible."

"We work pretty late sometimes. Could you make it about eight?"

"Only if you insist. Where would you like to go?"

"I don't know. It really doesn't matter. Why don't you surprise me?"

"I'll give it my best shot."

"You'd better. Nothing you do surprises me anymore."

"I'll keep that in mind. Pleasant dreams, Nan."

"Thank you. Sleep well, Robert."

They hung up without saying goodbye. Nan leaned back after she replaced the receiver and reached over to the opposite pillow as a smile lighted her face. She was going to see him again. He cared for her enough to be hurt when she didn't kiss him. He wanted her . . . and, God help her . . . she wanted him. She turned on her side. Whatever had possessed her to tell him that she slept on the right side of the bed? She turned off the light but before she lay down she slid to the other side of the bed. It felt all wrong, but she forced herself to remain in that position until she fell asleep.

When morning came she was back on the left side of the bed.

For the first time in months Nan would have given anything not to have to go to work. It would have been fun to stay home and do all the things women did to get ready for a special date. She might have even gone shopping for a new dress. The truth was that she didn't look forward to having to face Craig Martindale after the fiasco of their date the night before. She had expected to see him at the lodge as was customary, but when she got to work, one of the Continentals was parked near the edge of the parking lot at Pinnacle Realty.

Craig got out and came toward her. "Are you still speaking to me?"

"Of course. Did you think I wouldn't?"

He shrugged. "Can't say I'd blame you. William told me the bare details. I just want to tell you I'm sorry. This sort of thing never happens to me. There was a time I used to drink myself into a stupor but I haven't done that for years. I don't know what made me get carried away, but I'm sorry, Nan."

"You must have a dreadful headache this morning."

"It's bearable. William has a fantastic antidote, vodka and mineral oil and . . ."

Nan made a face. "Ugh. I don't want to hear about it so close to breakfast. Are you on your way up to the lodge?"

He nodded. "I came to ask you to ride up with me. The others have gone on ahead."

"Fine. I just have to stop in the office for a minute. You still haven't met my boss," she said as he opened the door for her. "I think you used to know her years ago."

"Oh yeah?" He didn't sound very interested but when he stepped inside, Laura was just coming out of her office. They both stopped dead. Nan could have sworn that his face turned white.

"Laura Lee, is that you?"

"Hello, Craig. It's been a long time."

"My God. I'd given up ever seeing you again." He went over to her and put his arms around her. "You look great, Laura Lee, just great."

"The years have been good to you too, Craig. You've come a long way since we worked together at United Artists."

"What happened to you after we split up? I looked all over Hollywood and half of L.A. for you."

"It's a long story, Craig, and we've both got work to do. Maybe some other time."

He drew back as if he had been hit in the face with a bucket of ice water. "Oh. Sure, whatever you say . . . some other time." With that he turned and walked out the door.

Laura went into her office, closing the door after her, and Nan was left standing at the desk with her mouth open. The air was still charged with the electricity of their meeting. There was a whole lot more to the story than Laura had led her to believe, no mistake about that. After a moment's indecision about whether to try to see if Laura was all right Nan finally decided to let things lie. She picked up her briefcase and a note pad and followed Craig out to the Continental.

He hardly seemed to hear her close the door as she got in. "Are you sure you want me to ride with you?" she asked. "Maybe you'd rather be alone?"

"Huh . . . oh, no." He turned the key and revved the motor. Shifting into reverse, he spun the wheels in a tight arc and scattered gravel as he exited the parking lot.

"Okay. Let's have it. How long has she been working here?"

"Seven years, I think. She's the owner of the agency. Before she got her broker's license she worked for another agency as an agent."

"And before that?"

"I don't know. Laura never talks much about the past. She did say that she had been in a couple of movies quite a few years ago."

"Did she know I was coming here?"

"Yes. I told her. She mentioned that she had known you slightly in the past."

"Slightly! My God." He was silent for a while. "Didn't she act like she wanted to see me?"

Nan was at a loss for words. She moved uncomfortably in the seat. "We really have been too busy to talk very much these last few days. But I feel sure she wanted to see you again. Before I found the lodge I was tempted to give up but she insisted we find a location for you."

He laughed harshly. "Sure, why not? She made a bundle on the commission."

Nan reached over to touch his arm. "You're wrong. I think it was more than that. Call it intuition, but I feel sure Laura wanted very much to see you again."

The car slowed perceptibly as he turned to search her face. "Look, don't snow me just because you think it's what I want to hear. How come she hasn't made the scene before now? I've been around the office several times. It seems funny that I didn't run into her before this."

"I wondered about that too, until now." She put her hand on his arm. "It's been what, Craig, ten years? She must have aged considerably during that time. Do you know what that means to a woman? It must be even worse for a woman who made her living in front of a camera."

"Well, time hasn't exactly stood still for me, either."

"Oh come on! In our society, men improve with age. Once a woman passes eighteen, she's made to feel that she can never again be as desirable as she was at that time. Granted, it's partly a state of mind, but every woman has to face the crisis of growing older. If she loves someone, she wants him to think of her as young and beautiful—not beautifully preserved."

He nodded. "Even if what you say is true, there were a good many years when she was still young that she could have come back to me."

"She never talked about those years, so I don't know what happened." She turned to face him. "But you could ask her. Maybe she had a good reason."

"Hah. I can think of a dozen but it doesn't make me feel any better. Just forget I ever mentioned it. We were two ships that passed in the night."

They rode in silence until they turned in to the parking area at the lodge. Nan was unable to get used to the change that had taken place almost overnight. Once quiet and pastoral, the area surrounding the lodge bustled with activity. A number of camper-trailers had been parked on the drive to serve as dressing rooms, offices, and prop rooms for the crew. An oversize trailer was set up as kitchen to provide light meals and a steady supply of coffee and doughnuts.

As if sensing Craig's mood, the crew and cast, in costume and makeup, assembled without the usual repetition of calls over the loud speaker. Craig drove them and himself harder than on any of the previous days. It was as if he were trying to exorcise his own private collection of devils. They went through "take" after "take" until everyone was tense and irritable.

Craig jumped up out of his chair wearing irritation like a second skin. "Cut!" He swore ceaselessly as he strode over to where the supposed villain was sneaking in through the glass doors. "Freddie, you're supposed to be breaking into the house, not walking across a golf course. This scene has less suspense than waiting for bread to rise. Go on outside and try it again."

"Scene five, take nine," the voice intoned wearily. "Action . . . roll 'em."

This time Freddie made a frighteningly real approach to the glass doors but somehow the catch had snapped into place and, when he tried to open them, he was locked out.

"Cut." There was a general groan from the people in the room and then when the latch was released Craig droned out, "Try it again."

Nan's back had begun to ache from the long day of comparative inactivity but when she looked at her watch she was appalled to see that it was after seven. Robert was supposed to pick her up at eight. She'd barely make it even if they left now, and Craig showed no sign of taking a break. The telephones in the house had not been connected, but she knew that the limousine had a mobile phone.

Dashing outside she asked William to let her make a call. She called the King Midas and asked to be connected with Robert's suite but the phone rang for several minutes and no one answered. In desperation she spoke to the girl at the switchboard.

"Do you know where I can reach Mr. Easton? This is Nan Gilliam. It's very important."

"No, Miss Gilliam. He left word that he would be home later tonight. Would you like to leave a message?"

"He was supposed to pick me up at eight but I won't be able to make it home on time. Surely you must have some idea where he might be?"

"Shall I ring his office in the Annex?"

"Oh yes, please."

There was no answer. Nan let it ring a dozen times while she tried to think what to do. "Could you ring the garage?" she asked when the operator came back on the line. "Maybe I can reach Arthur, his chauffeur."

He answered immediately.

She could hardly keep her hands from shaking. "Arthur, this is Nan Gilliam. You took me home from the casino last night..."

"Yes, Miss Gilliam. Is there something I can do for you?"

"I'm supposed to meet Mr. Easton at my house at eight but I'm still up at the lodge and won't be able to get back in time. I've tried everywhere but can't seem to find him to let him know. Do you have any idea where he is?"

"I wish I could help. He told me that he wouldn't be needing the car tonight, but the Maserati is gone—so I assume he drove himself. Have you tried the office?"

She groaned. "I've tried everywhere I can think of."

"If he comes in, I'll tell him that you called. In the meantime, I'll ask around to see if anyone knows where to locate him."

"Thank you, Arthur. If I'm not at home I can be reached

at the mobile phone." She gave him the number then hung up
and thanked William for the use of the phone. They were still
working on scene five when she got back.

Fifteen minutes later they were working on the layup for
another scene. "Come on with that lighting," Craig yelled.
"I need a sunset slanting across the floor through the glass
doors by the deck."

Without thinking Nan spoke up. "You can't do that, Craig."

"Why the hell not? It's sure not going to hurt your precious
floors."

She swallowed. He really must be tired. It was a rare thing
for him to be temperamental on the set. "I . . . I'm sorry. I
didn't mean it was going to hurt the floor."

"Well what is it then?" His voice was ragged with exhaustion.

She kept her voice low. "The deck overlooks Lake Tahoe
to the east. You can't have a sunset coming in the window.
It would have to be a sunrise."

"So . . . the house is on the other side of the lake."

"But the script said California. The other side of the lake
would put the house in Nevada."

When she heard his reaction she was almost sorry she had
told him. He had a vocabulary of swear words she had never
dreamed existed. When he finally cooled down he dropped into
a chair.

"Let's wrap it up for today. I don't know about the rest of
you, but I'm beat." They all agreed and began to disband before
he had a chance to change his mind. Ten minutes later Nan
had locked the building and was waiting for Craig to return
from one of the trailers for the ride back to town.

Just as she entered the front door of her house the phone
was ringing. She glanced at her watch as she ran to answer it.
Three minutes after nine. Robert would be furious.

She picked up the receiver. "Hello, Robert?"

"Miss Gilliam, this is Arthur. I still haven't located Mr.
Easton. I've tried every place I can think of but without success."

She tried to keep the disappointment from her voice. "I
can't tell you how much I appreciate all you've done. When

you see him would you please ask him to call me? Tell him it's very urgent."

"Yes, ma'am, I'll surely do that."

She started to hang up but heard him say something. "Yes, Arthur, was there something else?"

"Well...this is really a remote possibility but I just happened to think about the boat. He hasn't been down there in weeks so I don't think it's worth checking into."

"Which marina does he use?"

"The one over by Tahoe Keys, but I don't think you can reach them by phone this time of night."

"What does his boat look like?"

"Oh, you couldn't miss it. It's a thirty-footer, a white hull with a globe and eagle painted on it...you know, like at the entrance to the lodge."

"Thanks. I'm going to drive over there on the chance that I'll find him. After that I'll come straight home in case you hear from him first."

She didn't take time to change clothes. Grabbing her purse she dashed out the front door, unlocked the garage, and backed out at the same time hitting the button to activate the Genie. She didn't even wait to see if it closed.

Traffic was a mess. Everyone was headed toward Stateline and the casinos and was taking his own sweet time about it. She gave a beep to the horn but it only made the man in the car ahead of her slow down. As they pulled up to the red light Nan swung into the other lane and jumped the light an instant before it turned green. Then, cutting to the left she got in front of him as he laid on the horn and gave a one finger salute while he yelled something obscene about women drivers.

She caught the next light on the yellow and swung her car left into Tahoe Keys Boulevard. A quick glance into the rearview mirror sent a cold chill down her legs. A police car was right behind her. She leaned back and tried to look relaxed as she eased up on the accelerator. All she needed to make this a perfect day was a ticket for reckless driving. She hadn't broken any laws—maybe bent them a little, but hardly enough to merit a ticket. The cop stayed on her tail for another two blocks of pure unadulterated anxiety. Just as she made the turn

onto Venice, he swerved off with a friendly beep on the horn.
"I'd like to give you a beep or two," she snarled.

Pushing the accelerator as hard as she dared, Nan braked
to slow down as she turned into the marina lot and saw Robert's
car parked at the end of a pier. She pulled up alongside it and
got out, closing the door quietly behind her. The pier looked
deserted except for a few lights in some of the larger boats.
She walked down the length of a dock and finally spotted his
boat tied up at a slip on the other side. There was a light burning
in the cabin. With growing impatience she retraced her steps
until she reached the right dock. There was no wind. The boats
lay at their moorings, silent as the bird resting atop a channel
marker just outside the marina.

Suddenly she began to regret her impetuous decision to go
looking for him. What if he were angry that she chased him
down? Worse yet, what if he were not alone?

She gritted her teeth. It was too late now. She had practically
run afoul of the law to get here in a hurry. This was no time
to turn back. Maybe she could peek inside without his knowing
she was there. Then if he were with someone, she could leave
without him being the wiser. She took off her shoes and stepped
aboard the yacht. It was larger and more impressive than she
had expected. Ducking her head, she went down a short stairway which led to the cabin. The light had been in the first
porthole on the right and the door stood partway open.

He was alone, lying on the narrow bunk with his hands
tucked behind his head. So far he seemed unaware that she was
aboard.

He sat up as she tapped on the door.

"Who is it?" There was no sign of welcome in his voice.

Pushing the door the rest of the way open, Nan stepped
inside. Suddenly she didn't know what to do next.

He swung his feet over the side of the bed and ran his fingers
through his hair. "Let's have it. I can't wait to hear your
explanation."

Her heart went out to him. He looked absolutely wretched.
"I had to work late. We didn't finish filming until nearly nine."

"You could have left a message at the hotel."

"I did. The girl at the desk told me she'd pass it along."

"Jimmy Jackson works the desk tonight."

"Not when I called. Do you think I'm lying?"

He sighed. "No. You're painfully honest. I was just finding it hard to get over my earlier disappointment. I waited all day for eight o'clock when I could pick you up."

She felt something melt inside her. "Don't give me too much credit for honesty. I lied to you last night."

He looked up warily. "Oh? Would you care to tell me about it?"

She ran a quick tongue across her lips. "I . . . I told you I sleep on the right side of the bed."

He looked at her with slowly dawning comprehension and, for the first time that night, he smiled.

Chapter Eight

HE PUT HIS hand down on the bunk to steady himself. Then as if afraid to believe what he had heard he stood facing her. "What did you just say?"

"Don't pretend you didn't hear. I know you did and I refuse to repeat it."

He started to smile and slowly, deliberately, he lifted his arms toward her and equally as slowly, Nan walked into them. He held her for a long time as if to savor the way she felt against his chest. His face brushed across the top of her head.

"Your hair smells delicious, like bayberry."

He pressed her closer against him. "When I went to pick you up and your house was dark I was convinced that you had been leading me on last night simply as a way of getting even. I called your office but it was closed. I knew the lodge phone wasn't connected, so I called the mobile phone operator but she refused to give me the number."

"Um. They were deluged with calls from would-be actors

76

and had to have the number changed. I'm sorry. I did give the number to your secretary but I should have given it to you."

"Why did you tell me you sleep on the right side of the bed?"

"I . . . I don't know. I think I was afraid for you to know too much about me, the personal things. It was as if you were trying to move into my life all in one day and I wasn't sure I was ready for you."

"Then what made you change your mind? You did change it, didn't you?"

She didn't answer but lifted her chin and looked into his eyes. Slowly he reached down and cupped her face in his hand as his mouth found hers. His kiss was incredibly warm and sweet, gentle but commanding as he led and she followed through each new element of tasting and touching. The soft rasp of his mustache against her lips stirred her senses until she responded with an eagerness she would rather have concealed.

Breathless at last he held her at a distance. "I've waited a long time for that." He nodded toward the bed. "We could be more comfortable over there."

"I know . . . but it's too soon. I'm sorry."

"So am I."

She smiled. "And you did say you like to take things slow and easy."

He twisted his mouth into a wry smile. "Not one of my favorite quotable quotes, I'm afraid."

She stepped away from him and walked toward the door. "I'm sorry about our date. Would you like to make it some other time?"

"Anything wrong with right now?"

"Not if you'll give me a chance to freshen up. I made such a mad dash to get here that I didn't stop to comb my hair or wash my hands. Also . . ." She looked down at her blue and gold plaid shirt and jeans. "I'm really not dressed for a date."

"You look great, Nan. Besides, I was going to suggest we take the boat out on the lake. The galley is stocked for a feast. We could spend a week out there without having to return."

She gave him a look. "If you'll settle for dinner and a moonlight cruise, you're on."

He stepped into the companionway. "The head is the second door on the left. Make yourself comfortable while I get us underway."

The interior of the boat was paneled in a medium tone of pecky cypress. She followed the narrow corridor past the open doorway to a smaller cabin. The head was less spacious than she had imagined it could be, but bathtub, shower, sink, and commode were fitted in so perfectly that it didn't seem crowded. A mirror stretching across one side of the cubicle gave the feeling of added space. She ran a comb through her hair, splashed water on her face, and added a touch of lipstick. A short time later she went in search of Robert, who had adjusted the big diesel engine to a powerful sounding idle while he untied the lines.

Once the lines were coiled on board he went to the cockpit and turned on the running lights. "All set?" he asked.

"Whenever you are." She took the white padded leatherette seat next to him where he sat behind the wheel.

Shifting into reverse and easing forward on the throttle, Robert slowly backed the boat out of its mooring slip and then turned to enter the channel. Nan left her seat to reach over the side to bring the bumpers aboard.

"It's so beautiful, isn't it, with the reflection from the condominiums shining on the water? Look, you can see the lights in the tram as it comes down off the mountain."

"Probably people coming down after having dinner at the Top of the Tram. Is there any place you'd like to go?"

"No. Being on the water is enough for me." She went to stand behind him where he sat at the wheel. "It's the closest thing to paradise as far as I'm concerned."

"I don't know about you, but I'm starved. Let's anchor offshore while we see what there is for dinner."

A short time later he cut the engine and Nan climbed up on the bow and made ready to drop the anchor as soon as they drifted to a stop. As she started to step down he came forward and lifted her against him until her toes just touched the main deck. She wound her arms around his neck and brushed his face with her lips. "I thought you were starved."

He laughed. "It isn't my first choice, but I have the feeling you've already made up your mind that we're going to have dinner."

"It sounds like a fine idea. Do I cook or do you?"

"We both do. That lobster I promised you is waiting in the fridge." He let her go with apparent reluctance. "We can broil it in the tabletop broiler oven."

He had picked up some twice-baked potatoes and a carton of coleslaw from the restaurant at the King Midas. The potatoes and a foil container of buttered carrots went into the waist-high oven along with some tiny pumpernickel rolls. Robert broiled the lobster while Nan set the table with blue and ivory plates in a nautical pattern which was repeated on the heavy mugs.

They were sitting over their coffee when Nan put her cup down and looked around. "I can see why you laughed when I offered to take you for a ride in my rowboat. This is really fabulous. Have you taken any long trips with it?"

"Not yet. I haven't had the time. I'd like to take it up to Seattle and then cruise the inner passage between Canada and Alaska. It's only in the last six months that I've had any time to even think about taking a trip. After my father died it took me quite a while to learn the business enough so that I could leave the details to selected directors."

"From what I hear, the company is doing well. You're pretty famous around town for your innovative enterprises."

"I have a competent group of people working for me."

She clicked her tongue. "Such modesty."

He shot a glance in her direction. "Careful, you're living dangerously, unless you happen to be a long-distance swimmer."

She lifted her chin. "Don't be too sure of yourself. It might be you in the water and me behind the wheel. I know enough about boats to make it to shore."

"Not this one, you don't. It's programmed to go down with the captain."

She laughed. "All right, you win. I'll try to stay on my good behavior." She stretched and yawned. "I'll have to admit that you have a way with lobster. I've never tasted anything so delicious in my life."

"Your steak last night was better. You have a lovely home."

"I like it, too, although most of the credit goes to my parents. They built it and furnished it. I inherited it and have been trying to keep it in reasonably good condition."

"It must be hard having to work and take care of a house at the same time."

She laughed. "That's women's liberation. We have the right to have another job along with cooking and cleaning and minding the kids."

"Kids?"

She looked over at him, then laughed. "Well, in a manner of speaking. I don't have any children if that's what you mean."

"Would you like to?"

"Yes, three, if possible, providing I find the right man for a husband."

"I take it Lance Hendricks wasn't that man?"

"No. He has enough emotional problems of his own without taking on children to raise."

"Is that why you divorced him?"

She looked down at the table. "Partly. Lance wasn't ready for marriage. He was bent on a path of self-destruction and at the rate he was going, it wouldn't have taken long. He is convinced he can do everything better than anyone else, and it didn't matter that he put his life on the line each time he tried. First there was hang-gliding, then the demolition derby. He nearly killed himself during that phase. It was months before he was able to walk again. After that he took up auto racing. I couldn't take it any longer. I was constantly nervous and irritable. I finally gave him an ultimatum and when that failed, we divorced." She shrugged. "At first I wondered if I had done the right thing, but seeing him the way he is now, there's no doubt in my mind. He's started gambling . . . something he never did while we were married . . . unless you count gambling with his life. He's changed so much since the divorce that it's almost frightening."

He reached for her hands across the table. "I'm sorry, Nan, but I had to know. Are you over him now?"

"I was over him six months before I divorced him. He has his own place. I rarely see him anymore. I didn't ask him for alimony so I don't have any ties to him. That's one reason I took back my maiden name." She returned the pressure of his fingers. "The only time I see Lance is when we have business to discuss. When he refused to get psychiatric help I decided there was nothing more I could do for him."

He pulled her to her feet and around the side of the table until they were facing. "There is something you can do for *me*."

She stared up at him. "If you think I'm going to ask what, you're crazy."

He shook his head. "A hard woman. I guess I'll have to clear the table by myself."

She gave him a playful jab in the ribs. "I'll get you for that, Robert Easton." She slowly drew her hands away from his. "I put a kettle of water to boil on the hot plate. It must be ready by now. I'll wash, you dry."

"Slave driver. I should put you in charge of my staff at the Golden Slipper Club."

He tuned the portable radio to an FM station, which was playing dance music from the forties. After the dishes were cleaned and stowed in the proper compartment Robert brought cushioned lounge chairs onto the stern section of the deck so they could relax and look at the stars. A slight breeze had sprung up, causing the boat to drift slowly around the anchor. Nan closed her eyes, letting the motion soothe her into a state of drowsiness.

"Um." She sighed. "This must be what it feels like to sleep on a water bed. I may never get up."

"You don't have to, you know. We could spend the night out here on the water."

That woke her up. She turned her head toward him. "I appreciate the offer, but I'll pass."

"Don't get excited. There's an extra cabin. You can have a bed all to yourself."

She felt contrite. "I shouldn't have jumped to conclusions. I'm sorry I misjudged you, Robert."

He laughed. "Don't be too sorry. The idea did cross my mind. You'll have to admit it's hard to find a more romantic setting."

She fixed him with her gaze. "Was this what you had in mind all along...dinner for two followed by a moonlight cruise?"

"You said you wanted to be surprised."

"I guess we were both surprised. I couldn't have enjoyed it more, but I really should be going home."

He stood up. "It's early. Let's dance." He reached for her hand and pulled her up out of the deck chair. She went slowly into his arms, knowing that to risk the pleasure of his touch was to court danger. She closed her eyes. The danger was so beautifully tempting . . . so exquisitely exciting.

He bent his head and traced his mouth along her forehead, across her cheek and down the length of her throat. Lifting her hair he mouthed the back of her neck, sending warmth flooding through her veins.

"I . . . I thought we were going to dance," she stammered.

"Would you rather?"

Nan waited a long time before she answered. When she did, it was a whisper. "No . . . no." She reached her arms upward and wound them around his neck. Grasping the back of his head in her hand she forced it downward until she could reach his mouth, then kissed him with all the urgency of passion too long denied.

He groaned, pulling her hips into the arc of his legs until she knew the strength of his desire, then held her there against him, trembling and weak.

"Are you sure you don't want to stay here tonight?" His voice was husky and low.

"At this moment I'm not even sure who I am."

He hesitated as if considering her reply. "I'd like to take that to mean you want to stay but I have a terrible feeling that it means no."

"I don't know, Robert. I'm so confused. Don't force me to decide."

"One of us has to. If we go on much longer there is no way I can stop."

"I know."

"It's not as if anyone would know . . ." he reasoned.

"But we would, wouldn't we?"

He laughed harshly. "In a manner of speaking." He dropped his arms and walked away. "Okay. We'll do it your way."

Unsure of what he meant, Nan followed him only to discover that he had unhooked his belt and was working on the button at the top of his pants. A warning signal flashed in her brain and she looked wide-eyed at him.

He laughed. "Don't hit the panic button. I'm going for a swim. If you aren't ready for the shock of your life you'd better turn around."

She felt her face go scarlet and was grateful for the darkness which partly concealed it. She cleared her throat. "Dear Lord, Robert, you'll freeze! The lake must be like ice."

"It had better be." It sounded as if he spoke through clenched teeth. Seconds later she heard the splash of water against the hull as Robert dived overboard. When he came up, he caught his breath in a strangled gasp then swam a few desperate strokes toward the ladder.

Nan went down to the head and returned with a huge beach towel which she threw toward him as he climbed over the rail. While he got dressed she went below to comb her hair and touch up her lipstick, but she tried to avoid looking at herself in the mirror. Her eyes were still dark with the need for him and she didn't know quite what to do about it.

Although they tried, neither of them could recapture the feeling of easy camaraderie they had known on the way out. Robert's jokes were a little flat and everything Nan said seemed to have a double meaning. After a while they fell silent, content just to look at each other in the faint glow of the panel light.

Once the boat was tied up at the mooring, Robert followed Nan over to her car and held the door until she got in. He bent down and brushed his mouth against hers.

"I'll follow in my car."

"I don't think that's a good idea."

He swore softly. "Look, Nan. I just want to make sure you get home all right. The last two times we had a date you walked home. I'd like to make sure that doesn't happen again."

She smiled, remembering past misunderstandings. Thank heaven they knew each other better now. "All right." She grinned. "Try to keep up with me."

He was still shaking his head when he got into his car. She started her car and waited for the throb of his engine before she backed out of the lot.

It was strange. Even in their separate isolation she could feel the bond between them which distance could not diminish.

Would he try to follow her into the house once she arrived home? And if he did . . . would she have the strength to refuse him? After all, she wasn't an innocent girl. Was it so wrong to give and receive the pleasure which could only come from the ultimate gift? Her parents had never preached to her about the sanctity of the body. Instead, they had tried to instill in her the profound joy that came from self-respect. They were convinced that contentment was the perfect happiness and self-respect was its parent. They taught by example, and the result of their teachings was a set of values which she cherished.

She blinked back the tears. It had always been easy to live up to their standards . . . until now. She looked into the rearview mirror. Twin headlights burned through the faint mist which was beginning to roll across the ground. It was as if he were staring at her, demanding a response, giving her no choice but to surrender to him.

He could have taken her, willing or unwilling, at any time, had he wanted to. God . . . she almost wished he had. That way the burden would have been on him. Instead, he chose to play the martyr. It occurred to her that she, too, should have gone for a swim. He, at least, was in no apparent discomfort.

She jerked the car to the right to avoid an approaching vehicle. Thank heaven she was nearly home. It was next to impossible to concentrate on the road.

As she got out of her car she waited for Robert to pull alongside. "There is no need for you to get out. We can say goodnight here."

"Oh? Maybe you can but I can't. Come on. I'll see you to the door."

"Robert . . ." she said appealingly.

He gave her a look. "Don't worry. The door is as far as I go."

She smiled and handed him her key. As he reached for the doorknob the door pushed open.

"Hey, it's not even locked."

"But I always keep my door locked. Could someone have broken in?"

"We'll soon find out. You stay here. I'll have a look inside."

"No. I'm coming with you." She followed close behind. "Shall we turn on the lights?"

"We might as well. With as much noise as we were making we couldn't hope to surprise anyone."

She reached for the wall switch. "The living room looks all right. It doesn't look like they touched anything. I don't get it. If it were a thief he'd surely have taken the silver candelabra. They're worth quite a bit."

"If someone did try to break in they might have been frightened off before they had a chance to take anything. I'll look in the family room and kitchen. You stay here."

She went to her bedroom door and looked in to find Lance, his clothes strewn all over the floor, sound asleep in her bed. Her first instinct was to keep Robert from finding out, and she went with it, closing the door softly behind her.

Robert came down the hall toward her and opened the door to a spare bedroom then went in to check the closet. "Nothing so far, not even a sign that anyone was here. You must have forgotten to lock the door." He started to go toward her bedroom. "Do you keep the door to your room closed?"

"No, I . . . that is I've checked it."

He looked at her oddly then continued on. "I'll check it again. You may have missed the closet."

She moved to block his way. "No. It's all right, Robert."

He stopped dead in his tracks. "Do you open it or do I?"

She put her hands on his chest. "Please don't go in. It's Lance. Somehow he must have gotten into the house. He's sleeping."

"In your bed?"

"I . . . yes."

"That's great, just great! God, Nan, you must take me for a fool. All that talk about it being all over between the two of you . . ." He ran his fingers through his hair. "And I believed you. What'd you do? Leave a key under the mat?"

"No. I must have left the door unlocked when I dashed off to find you."

"A Freudian slip, maybe? Were you hoping he'd come back to you?" He opened the door and looked in. "At least he knows which side of the bed to sleep on. It looks like he was expecting you."

Nan knew what he meant. Lance had found her black lace nightgown in the drawer and draped it over the foot of the bed.

She closed the door quickly and, grabbing Robert by the arm, half dragged him into the hallway.

"Please don't do this, Robert. When you have time to think it over you'll know that I told you the truth. He's probably trying to get back at me for starting to date again. Lance loves to play games. This is just the sort of thing that would appeal to his sense of humor. I can handle him. I'll wake him up and send him home, but it will be easier if you aren't here."

He grabbed her and dragged her against him. "Damn! I should have taken you when I had the chance. You won't spend the night on my boat but you have no qualms about spending the night alone with Lance." He was breathing hard and his voice sounded tight in his throat. "Well, fortunately he's sleeping on his own side of the bed. You won't have to have him move over."

Nan's face went white. "You shouldn't have said that. I'm sorry this had to happen, but what really hurts is that you are so unwilling to see it from my point of view. What I told you is true. It's over between Lance and me. If you choose to think otherwise . . . there is nothing left for us to say."

His face tightened as he put his hands on her shoulders.

Chapter Nine

ROBERT HELD HER so tightly that she couldn't move. "I under-estimated you, Nan. You got what you wanted, my signature on the lease. I think I'd better cut and run before you set your goals a little higher."

She swallowed, trying to keep her voice even. "When you've had time to think it over, Robert, you're going to feel like a fool for having said that. You signed the lease days ago. If what you said were true I'd have had no reason for chasing after you tonight." She blinked rapidly. "I'm sorry Lance is here, sorry for more reasons than you know, but he's here through no fault of mine and I can assure you that he won't be staying."

She thought she saw a softening of his expression, but Lance chose that moment to call out.

"Nan, baby. Come on to bed."

Robert swore in disgust and, pushing her aside, turned and strode from the house. Nan watched his car spin free of the driveway and saw his taillights disappear down the road. Turning slowly, she retraced her steps to the bedroom to confront Lance, but he was leaning against the doorway as she came down the hall.

"Don't tell me your date left already. Things were just beginning to get interesting." He grinned innocently. "You look steamed. Did your rich new friend say something to set you off?"

"Damn you, Lance. Just what are you doing here?"

"Hey . . . is that any way to treat me after all we meant to each other? I thought we had an amicable divorce."

"'Divorce' is the key word, Lance. It's over, finished, kaput. So why are you here?" Her words sounded as if they were chipped from a glacier.

He came toward her and put his hands on her arms. "I didn't feel like going back to the apartment. There's plenty of room here. It's not as if I were putting you out. Besides, I missed you, babes."

She moved away from him. "How come you didn't go to work? You're dressed for it."

He tucked his shirt into his pants then reached for his necktie. "I got all dressed to go but I called in sick. Morey Weinberg is sitting in for me tonight. It was a nothing show anyway; a juggler, a creep with a musical saw, and an animal act. Geez, I can face anything but an animal act."

"You're going to lose your job if you keep that up."

"Forget it, babes. They can't get along without me and they know it."

"I don't want you here, Lance. Now or ever again."

"Hostile, baby, purely hostile."

"I mean it. You put me in an embarrassing position by being here. What's more, I think you did it deliberately."

He grinned. "What a gas. Did what's-his-face get a look at me sleeping in your bed?"

Her face flamed as she went over to the telephone and picked it up. "If you aren't out of here in three minutes flat I'm calling the police."

"Aw come on. Don't be a sore loser. It was just a gag."

"I mean it, Lance."

He came over and put his arms around her. "Hey, baby,

don't be so cold. How can you forget all the good times we had together? Remember the trip we took down to Baja in the camper right after we got married?"

He pulled her close and slid his hands down to her waist and brought his face close to hers. "We could have it all again. I made a royal mess of things when I walked out on you, but I'd like to try again."

She shook her head. "You were right before, Lance, when you said you couldn't stand the routine of marriage. It can't possibly work for us. I wouldn't dream of asking you to try."

"I'm volunteering." He grinned as he kissed her in a pathetic attempt to kindle a spark, but she was unmoved. He looked at her closely, comprehension dawning on his face. "You've been sleeping with that turkey, haven't you? Oh, don't bother to deny it. No wonder I get nothing but the cold shoulder.

"Look, Nan, if it's that Craig Martindale you might as well forget him. He's strictly first-cabin, babes. He picks his broads out of a smorgasbord line."

"If that's all you have to say, you might as well leave now, Lance, and don't expect the house to be unlocked next time. It'll never happen again, I guarantee it."

He held up his hands in mock alarm. "Okay, okay. I just tried to do you a favor. I hate to see you get hurt." A short time later he had backed his car out of the garage and sprayed a shower of gravel as he turned toward South Lake Tahoe.

More exhausted than she had been in weeks, Nan changed the sheets on the bed, took a hot shower, and was asleep within a half-hour.

The next morning she rose unrested and went into town to try to see Laura before she had to report to the lodge. As luck would have it, Laura was alone. Nan went into her office and sat down, running her fingernail along the groove in the top of the desk as she spoke the usual banalities while trying to assemble her thoughts. Finally, she folded her hands in her lap.

"About yesterday, Laura. . . . I'm sorry I brought Craig into the office without a little warning. I just didn't realize you had been involved with him. I had no idea your seeing him would create an awkward situation."

Laura shrugged. "Forget it. It was bound to happen sooner

or later." She swiveled her chair and pretended to be looking for something in her desk drawer. "What'd he say after you left?"

Nan took a deep breath. "Well . . . for one thing, he was extremely upset. It was obvious that he cared . . . and I think still cares for you very deeply. He was hurt that you never tried to keep in contact with him."

"He's got a short memory. I called him every day for a month and wrote him twice a week, but he never returned my calls or answered my letters."

"Maybe he never received them."

"Oh come on. I can see that happening four or five times— but not that many. No. He's just trying to save face. You saw how quick he took off after he saw me yesterday."

"Well, face it Laura, you hardly gave him any encourage- ment. You did everything but slam the door in his face."

"That never stopped Craig Martindale before. If he wants something, he takes it," she said with obvious pride.

Nan looked at her closely. "You're in love with him, aren't you?"

Laura snorted in her own peculiar way. "You're out of your mind. He's nothing but a wheeler-dealer who thinks he's the cock-of-the-walk. He's married to his work, can't hold his liquor . . . and unfortunately, has a heart of gold. I suppose there was a time when I loved him but . . . well, we all have to grow up."

Nan looked at her steadily. "I find it odd that neither of you ever married."

"Don't try to make it the romance of the century. We had something great while it lasted, but it closed on the road. It never made the big time and it's been dead too long to try and revive it once the curtains came down."

Nan could tell that Laura no longer wished to discuss Craig. Since it was time for her to leave for the lodge, she used that as an excuse to end the conversation.

Because hers was the only key to the main building, she made it a point to arrive well ahead of the shooting schedule. The stars were already in their trailers being made up for the stairway sequence where Karen Shane was supposed to shove her grandfather, Gordon King, down the stairs. A stuntman would take the actual fall and makeup had their work cut out for them to make the men resemble each other. As she went up to unlock the door, Craig waved a greeting then gave orders for the camera crews to follow her in to get the crane into position for the high shots.

Notebook in hand, Nan went around the house checking conditions to be certain that everything was still in good order. There would no doubt be some damage outside to the gravel parking area where the trailers were set up, but a fresh load of gravel would make it look like new. Aside from a few black marks on the floor which the matting did not cover, the interior seemed to be in good condition. Downstairs, hanging planters had been added to the hot-tub room. One particularly beautiful staghorn fern, which was mounted on a circle of fibrous wood, was dripping water onto the floor. Nan called the props man who immediately took care of it.

Rehearsing for the complicated shot began a scant half-hour later. Craig was usually fairly easygoing but, whether it was the intricacy of the shot or his own personal problems, he seemed to be uninclined to forgive mistakes. Karen forgot her lines twice during the first half-hour and Cassie, Craig's go-fer, otherwise known as a production assistant, was less than quick about prompting her.

He got out of the director's chair and stood with his legs spread. "All right. You people are behaving like a bunch of kids at summer stock rehearsal. If we don't get this in the can today we're going to run over the shooting budget. Now if you think *I'm* ticked off, wait'll you see what Sherm will do to you." He motioned to the grip. "Bring that key light in a little closer toward the foot of the stairs. And be ready to roll with that porto-cam. We'll need a closeup of Gordon's face during his death scene." He went back to his chair and slowly lowered himself. "Ready up there, Karen, Gordon? We'll start with the line, 'You should have died out there on the desert, old man.'"

The signal was given to roll the cameras, and for a while Nan became absorbed in the action. But despite her determination not to think about him, Robert kept ghosting his way into her thoughts.

Why did it have to be that their dates always turned into a

fiasco before the night was over? There was no doubt in her mind that he enjoyed her company beyond the point of casual friendship, but when things began to get serious between them something always happened to set him off. They both had short fuses but that alone should not have been enough to do it. Was he perhaps going out of his way to make certain their attraction for each other never got beyond the first stages? Or was she unconsciously making things happen to cool his ardor?

Ridiculous! It wasn't her fault that Lance turned up so unexpectedly in her bed. No . . . it was just a series of unfortunate incidents which had caused their problems. Maybe it was better that it had ended before things had gone too far. As soon as the thought crossed her mind she pushed it aside. No! The excitement she felt when Robert kissed her was too precious to deny. No matter what happened between them, it was worth it just for that single shattering memory. She blinked her eyes to keep back the tears. Whoever it was who compared love to being on a roller coaster ride knew what he was talking about.

She stirred in the chair as they called again for quiet on the set and the cameras began to roll. The stuntman took the fall down the stairs quite easily but with such realism that Nan nearly cried out. Then the cameras were stopped and Gordon replaced him in the same prone position at the foot of the stairs. Special effects had rigged a dye capsule to break so that it looked as if he had a deep gash in his forehead. As Karen ran down the stairs and stood over his body, Gordon bit down on another capsule causing a quantity of "blood" to trickle from his mouth. The cameras converged on the scene as Karen stooped down and took an envelope from his jacket pocket.

Even from where Nan watched between the cameras and lighting equipment the drama was evident. Gordon's face looked ghastly as he milked his death scene to the limit. When the call to cut was given, she felt completely drained. She reached over to touch Craig's arm. "Am I wrong or was that last scene absolutely perfect?"

He grinned. "Not too shabby, but wait until you see a composite run in slow motion for the fall. It'll blow your mind."

Cassie got up out of her chair and moved between Nan and Craig so that Nan had to remove her hand. The dark-haired woman bent low and spoke to Craig in an intimate way. Nan hcard cnough to guess that he was less than pleased with her suggestion, and the girl went back to her chair with a hurt expression on her face. During the short time they had been working at the lodge Nan had seen enough to know that Cassie took a very possessive attitude where Craig was concerned.

From the talk that drifted around during the lunch break she gathered that they went back a long way and that at one time the motion picture community had assumed they either were secretly married or at least engaged. From where Nan stood, she had the feeling that Craig was having second thoughts and Cassie wasn't taking it very well.

It was easy to see why Hollywood was known for its short-term marriages. People were thrown together for weeks at a time. Even though the shooting schedule was rigorous, beginning at the crack of dawn for the stars and makeup crews and ending usually around six, they still managed to find time to get together between takes and at lunchtime. Karen Shane and her co-star Fred Bond obviously had something going. Gossip had it that Fred, or Freddie as he was usually called, was only given a part in the picture at Karen's insistence. It occurred to Nan that he didn't gain much as far as his career was concerned, because the meaty role belonged to Gordon.

Before she realized what time it was, Craig had given the order to cut and print. It had been by far the most interesting of all the shooting days and she told Craig so as they made ready to wrap it up. He seemed a little more relaxed than he had since seeing Laura at the office.

He stopped at the door of the trailer with the film cans in his arms. "Listen, Nan, what say we put on the dog tonight? Dinner and dancing at the Colony?"

"I don't know, Craig . . . it's been a long day."

To Nan's surprise, disappointment was written all over his face. He leaned against the frame of the door. "Come on . . . we all need to relax."

She shrugged. "Okay. Why not? That is, providing you take it easy on the drinks."

He raised his eyebrows. "Word of honor. I'll pick you up about eight, okay?"

"Fine."

"And, oh yeah..."

She laughed. "Don't tell me, I know. Wear something sexy."

"You've got it."

Nan toyed with the idea of making a run into town to shop for a new dress, but by the time she reached the stop sign at Emerald Bay Road she had decided to go with her old black. Later, as she pulled it out of the garment bag, she began to have second thoughts but by then it was too late. The dress, cut to reveal one shoulder in the Grecian style, was a little too chic for her, accounting for the fact that she had worn it only once. She knew that it would appeal to Craig, a fact which helped make up her mind. After all, he had gone out of his way since the crew arrived at the lodge to make sure that nothing was damaged, and she felt a certain gratitude toward him.

Actually, he was quite a nice man once you got through the slick, Hollywood veneer. He had an extravagant sense of humor and was, except when he had been drinking, extremely considerate.

She brushed her hair out long, then wound it into a Psyche knot at the back of her head, leaving a thick length of hair which was clustered with curls to dangle free. The style went well with the dress. Leaning close to the mirror, she sighed thankfully that her childhood smattering of freckles had all but disappeared to leave her skin looking like creamy porcelain. Black wasn't her best color since it tended to make her skin look pale, but a touch of blusher on her cheekbones took care of that.

A silver clip fastened the gown at the top of one shoulder and she selected a sterling charm bracelet as her only jewelry. It was one of her favorite treasures although she rarely wore it because it had a tendency to snag her hose. The charms, each one marking a remembered event in her life, jingled musically on her arm.

One thing about Craig. He left no doubt as to his feelings. Where Robert might have simply nodded his approval at her appearance, Craig let out a low howl. "Honey, you are class with a capital *K*. You have a funny way of combining innocence with sophistication and I think you look terrific. Let's take in the action at the Colonnade room tonight. Cassie already took care of reservations."

Nan had a moment's discomfort. Poor Cassie. How it must hurt to have to make arrangements for her man to take another woman to dinner.

Once they were on their way Nan had to reevaluate the situation. It didn't take her long to realize that the main reason Craig had asked her to dinner was to question her about Laura. He had made a pathetic attempt to be subtle in his questioning of her but she thought him pitifully transparent. He was obviously in love with Laura... and always had been.

After the usual hullaballoo when they entered the club they were seated at a table near the dance floor. While they sipped their drinks, Craig managed to skirt all around the subject of Laura and Nan decided to make it easy for him by telling him all he wanted to know, short of where Laura lived. She had an unlisted phone number which she gave only to friends and clients, and Nan decided it was up to Laura to choose whether or not he be given that information.

It was just after they had finished the main course when Nan laid down her napkin. "Craig. Why don't you stop this pussyfooting around and go see Laura? It's obvious you're still crazy about her, and I'd be willing to bet she cares a great deal about you."

"Forget it, kid. She walked out on me and never bothered to tell me where she was going."

"But she did. She told me that she wrote you and telephoned several times within the period of a month."

"The hell she did."

"I'd be willing to bet on it. She told me that you could have come to her at any time but you never answered and never called."

"Man, how could I? I didn't know where she was."

"Could someone have intercepted her letters and calls?"

"Hell, no. There was no one around but..." He nearly dropped his glass of wine. "Why that little..." A wide grin spread across his face. "Come on, let's dance. I feel too good to sit still."

He grabbed her wrist and whirled her onto the floor. As she

went into his arms Nan caught a glimpse of Robert on the floor
opposite them. He was dancing with a tall, cool-looking blonde
with hair the color of warm honey and a dress that clung to her
curves like melted butter.

Craig's mood was reflected in his dance; happy and uninhibited. Holding her tightly he whirled her around the perimeter
of the floor in a fast swing step that left her breathless. She
tried to keep her gaze fixed on his face to avoid eye contact
with Robert, should he pass by. Craig could hardly have been
aware of what was happening. He was obviously too involved
with his new-found happiness to think of anything else, in-
cluding propriety. He looked at Nan for a minute then threw
his head back and laughed. "Honey, you've given me the best
news I've had in ten years." With that he proceeded to kiss her
soundly on the mouth in front of the entire restaurant.

The kiss didn't go unnoticed. A small ripple of laughter
began on one side of the room and moved like a tide to the
other. She felt her face go red. "Please, Craig. You're embarrassing me. Let's sit down."

He grinned. "Whatever you say," he said as he maneuvered
her through the crowd and back to their table.

Nan, feeling as vulnerable as if her lipstick were smeared
from ear to ear, excused herself and made her way to the
powder room. When she finally came out, Robert was standing
alone in the corridor waiting for her. His eyes were dark with
barely concealed anger. "Hasn't anyone taken the trouble to
tell you that you're making a complete and utter fool of yourself?"

She tried to pass by him without speaking but he grabbed
her by the shoulders and held her immobile.

"Let me go, Robert."

"Not until I shake some sense into your head. He's no good
for you, Nan. Wasn't your mistake with Lance enough to temper your judgment?"

"What I do is no business of yours. Let me go."

He shook her by the shoulders until her arms flapped like
a rag doll's. As she stiffened, her wrist dragged across his front
and her bracelet snagged on his fly near the top of his pants.

She felt her face turn crimson as she tried to pull away but was hopelessly caught. He must have realized something was wrong from the wild-eyed expression on her face, and he loosened his grip.

She ran her tongue across her lips to moisten them. "I . . . it's my bracelet, Robert. It's . . . it's caught on . . . on your trousers."

As he looked down, Nan took malicious delight in seeing the tips of his ears turn red. "Well, pull it off!" he commanded.

"I can't. It'll tear your pants."

He swore soundly. "God! What did I ever do to deserve you?"

Chapter Ten

THE CORRIDOR WHERE they were standing was apparently the only access to another area just beyond the restrooms. Robert swore in frustration as several passers-by looked at them in amusement. He pulled sharply at the bracelet but neither it nor the trousers gave way.

"We've got to move. I'll be damned if I can accomplish anything with everyone staring at us."

Nan smiled sarcastically. "Would you care to step into the ladies' room?"

He looked completely done in as he grabbed her arm and marched her in that direction. "I've been in worse places. Let's get it over with."

As Nan preceded him into the powder room, her left arm bent behind her back, the pert, English attendant looked up at Robert in surprise.

"I say, wot's this? None o' that now. We don't need no

perverts comin' in 'ere. This is a 'igh class ladies' room."

Nan tried to look confident. "It's all right. We've had a little accident and the gentleman is helping me free my bracelet." Now that they were in the semi-privacy of the ladies' room, Nan was beginning to see the humor in the situation. She had to struggle to keep from laughing.

Robert fiddled with the catch. "How in the devil do you work this thing? It's worse than a child-proof prescription bottle."

"It's really very simple. All you do is line up the knobs and slide the end around."

"Then *you* do it."

Once again she turned to face him, and for a moment their gaze met. The desperation in his eyes sobered her somewhat and she bent to open the catch. But it wasn't as easy as she thought. "I'm afraid it's been jammed. It doesn't turn the way it's supposed to."

He looked over at the attendant. "Do you have a pair of scissors?"

"Oh indeed I do, sir. They're manicure scissors, but they cut just fine."

Nan looked at him in irritation. "Don't be silly, Robert. You can't just go hacking away at a perfectly good suit. Here. Let me do it." She caught hold of the bracelet with her right hand using her left wrist for leverage, and, after a few hard tugs, the bracelet broke from her wrist and was left dangling down the front of his pants. Rubbing her wrist, she moved quickly away. "Keep your jacket closed and no one will ever suspect you're wearing my bracelet on your pants."

He stood there, speechless. Nan shrugged. "Well, it's up to you if you want to stay in the ladies' room. As for me, I'm going back to my table. Craig is bound to wonder what's happened to me."

She nodded her thanks to the attendant and walked around Robert as if to avoid further contact. He must have come out of the ladies' room directly behind her because she had just gone a few yards down the corridor when she heard a group of women titter. Nan smiled. It served him right to be made a laughingstock. Next time maybe he'd pay attention to his own date and not try to run other people's lives.

Craig stood as she approached the table. "Are you all right? I was beginning to worry."

She couldn't resist it. "I tangled with an old friend. It took longer than it should have. I'm sorry."

He gave her a curious look as he sat down. "What happened to your bracelet? You didn't lose it did you?"

"No. It got caught on ... something and broke, but thank you for your concern." She suddenly felt like dancing, although she knew the real reason she wanted to be on the dance floor was to get even with Robert. Craig obligingly led her into the pattern of an old-fashioned foxtrot as Nan, slightly deflated, noticed that Robert and his cool blonde were leaving the club. Judging from her expression, his friend was less understanding than Craig about having been left alone at the table.

With Robert gone, some of the fun had gone out of the evening. Craig, too, seemed to have his mind on other things—Laura, no doubt—and they decided to make an early night of it.

When he saw Nan to her door and planted a fatherly kiss on her cheek, she looked up at him. "What's going to happen now?"

He grinned. "I was planning to get into my car and drive back to the hotel. Did you have something else in mind?"

She flushed. "No, silly. I meant with you and Laura. Now that you know she tried to get in touch with you after she left, you surely are going to try to straighten things out, aren't you?"

He shrugged. "I thought about it for quite a while and I haven't made up my mind. God! It was so long ago. She's probably nothing at all like I remembered her. We were kids, then ... just getting started. She loved me as I was and I don't know if she'd like what I am now."

"What can you lose by finding out?"

"Look, it's easy enough for you to say. You don't know what I went through. It's taken me all these years to get over her, and I don't want to be put through it again."

It occurred to Nan that he still wasn't over Laura, but she decided it was prudent to remain silent. A short time later he said goodnight and she went inside.

It took her a long time to get to sleep that night. She kept waiting for the phone to ring. Judging from past experiences with Robert, he seemed to enjoy a verbal skirmish over the telephone, but whether he was still out with his blonde, or whether he was too angry to talk to Nan, she didn't know. Whatever the reason, her intuition was wrong. He didn't call.

Work went according to schedule on the set the following day. Craig, in a pensive mood, was less than his usual dynamic self. Consequently, the crew relaxed considerably. They wrapped it up early and Nan was home by six-thirty, after making a quick stop at the grocery store. She was just putting the produce into the crisper when Laura called.

"I hate to bother you at night but I have some papers for you to take care of. Would you mind if I stopped by after dinner?"

"Yes, but why don't you come for dinner? I'd love to cook for someone besides myself."

"Tempting. You're sure you don't mind?"

"I'd love it. Come whenever you're ready. Let's plan to eat about seven-thirty."

Nan felt a decided lift to her spirits as she slipped into a floor-length cotton skirt with a peasant blouse. She had never minded being alone until now, but lately she found that Robert intruded into her thoughts a little too often for comfort. In just a matter of a few days he had become the pivotal force in her life. She needed him and her intuition told her that his need for her was equally as strong. They had such fun together when they weren't at odds with each other, and even when they were fighting it was far better than being without him. Could it be that the reason behind their disagreements could be their mutual frustration? The possibility that it was true sent a flood of warmth down her legs.

Understandably, it had been a shock for him to walk into her bedroom and find Lance in her bed. Most people . . . men or women, preferred to think that they didn't have to share the attention they received with another. Robert knew that she had been married but it was the timing that was unfortunate. Still, he could have been more understanding.

Nan sighed as she cut the seeds from the center of a green pepper and sliced it into triangles. She had stopped loving Lance long ago, months before she divorced him. Even then she had almost stayed with him out of pity, but pity caused more harm than good. What he needed could only come when he made peace with himself. She'd done the right thing when she divorced him but she wanted to be done with it. She wanted Robert . . . and a chance for the real happiness that she knew could come from the love of a good man.

And Robert *was* a good man! He was just so damned ready to jump to conclusions. And now he had his embarrassment to add to his problem. She thought about calling him and trying to straighten it out. But no . . . he had to come to her. It was his problem. She wouldn't push him.

The grill was hot and the meat was ready to go on the skewers by the time Laura arrived. She smiled at Nan with admiration. "You look like the perfect little housewife with your ruffled apron and a potholder in hand."

Nan laughed. "I'll take that as a compliment. Come on in. Would you like a glass of wine or something to drink while we're waiting for the steak-a-bobs?"

"Could we make it coffee? I'm about to have a caffeine fit. The office has been a madhouse the last few days. I've been out most of the time showing condos to the Arabs."

"Lookers or buyers?"

"A little of both. I guess you could say that things have definitely taken a turn for the better. By the way, the Vabrowski's bought the Nicholson place you showed them so many times."

"No kidding? Boy, I sure had them figured wrong. I thought they were serious when they kept holding out for a hundred fourteen thousand."

"Well . . . he brought in the check for the earnest money today. I went ahead and had him sign the contract for a hundred twenty-five." She grinned. "I wasn't about to wait around for him to change his mind again. Of course the commission is yours, but I hope I didn't have to tell you that."

"Thanks. I really appreciate your handling my clients while I'm up at the lodge."

"Forget it. I've got a few papers for you to sign but otherwise, everything's going smoothly."

They drank coffee and apple juice while the beef brochette with onions, tiny tomatoes, green pepper, and bacon broiled over the gas grill on the deck.

After dinner they lounged on the deck with tall glasses of orange sherbet whipped into a froth. Nan had been waiting all evening to find the right time to bring up the subject of Craig.

She turned to watch Laura. "I had dinner last night with Craig." Laura's gaze became hooded as Nan continued. "It was lovely. We spent the whole evening talking about you."

"Sounds dull to me," Laura said, obviously trying to keep the relief from her voice.

"I found out something. Craig never received your letters or phone messages. He thought you had walked out on him and cut all ties."

"He should have known better. But even so, he couldn't have been very concerned. He didn't bother to come after me."

"He tried. He didn't know where you were."

"I sent him my address."

"I have a feeling your letters were intercepted by his go-fer, Cassie Rinella. Have you ever heard of her?"

"Sure. She used to be a hanger-on . . . a two-bit prop girl back in those days. She always was after Craig."

"Well, she's production assistant now, but she acts like she owns Craig."

"Good for her."

"But the point is . . . she doesn't. Craig tolerates her and that's all. I think he's still in love with you, Laura."

"Me and a dozen other women."

"Maybe, but I don't think so. It's all show, or at least the image he tries to project. He keeps asking about you."

Laura got up and walked over to the railing to stare out at the lake. "Look, Nan. I appreciate what you're trying to do, but you don't know the whole story. It took me all these years to get over Craig. I don't want to go through it again."

"Funny. He said almost the same thing."

She laughed without amusement. "Well, for once we agree on something."

Nan looked carefully at Laura's face. "I didn't think you'd pass up a chance like this. Craig may have his tough, Holly-wood exterior, Laura, but deep down he's a very special man. His main problem is that his fame precedes him."

"He asked for it."

"Doesn't everyone in that kind of profession? How can you

be successful if people don't know who you are? The point is,
the Craig Martindale he shows to the public isn't the real Craig
Martindale. You of all people ought to know that."

Laura returned to her chair. "Let's drop it. This conversation
is going nowhere."

"Don't you ever miss the excitement of the motion picture
business? It's like living in a different world."

Laura nodded. "It's all that and more. Sure, I miss it, but
I discovered how nice it is not to have to duck the bill collector.
I'd never go back to acting, not even for a starring roll."

"But wouldn't you enjoy watching? I was hoping I could
talk you into going up to the lodge with me tomorrow."

Laura's eyes narrowed. "This wouldn't be a subtle ploy to
bring about a meeting between Craig and me?"

Nan smiled. "Well, I won't go so far as to say you could
avoid meeting him, but you don't have to do anything you
don't want to."

"I have to admit . . . I'd love to watch. Are you sure it will
be all right? Craig was always fussy about having strangers on
the set."

"You're hardly a stranger."

Laura gave her a look meant to wither but Nan could see
the suppressed excitement in the woman's eyes. It was a chance
she was taking, trying to get these two stubborn people together
again, but her intuition told her it was worth a try. She only
hoped her meddling wouldn't end in disaster.

The next day, Laura wasn't about to take unnecessary
chances. Rather than riding along with Nan up to the lodge,
she insisted on following in her own car. "I'm not sure I can
afford to spend the whole day up there," she insisted. "With
two of us away from the office, the whole place could fall
apart."

Once they had parked in the area next to the trailers, Laura's
eyes began to sparkle and her cheeks were flushed with excitement. "It's as if I've never been away. My stomach feels
the way it used to feel when I wasn't sure I had learned my
lines."

Nan squeezed her arm. "Don't worry. Everything's going

to be just fine. Take my word for it."

As it turned out, it was even better than Nan could have hoped. Craig was the gracious host, showing Laura around the set, explaining the plot and how the shooting had gone so far, and even discussing the merits of various special effects they planned to employ.

Nan breathed a sigh of relief. As far as she could tell they had as yet to discuss personal matters but she was confident they would get to that later on.

Cassie Rinella was livid. More than once she tried to separate Craig from his attention to Laura, but without success. Watching the dark-haired woman, Nan found it hard to believe that such a lovely girl had been guilty of preventing Craig's and Laura's reconciliation. And if she had, would she attempt another dirty trick?

If Cassie were down, Craig was the opposite end of the emotional pole and his good mood affected everyone around him. Without a doubt it was the most successful day of shooting they had completed up until then. By four o'clock they had finished their shooting schedule and to everyone's delight, Craig gave them until noon the following day to report.

Nan was alone with Laura for a few minutes during a break. Laura was alive with crackling excitement. "He asked me to go out with him tonight."

Nan gave her a hug. "Terrific. Where are you going?"

"That's just it. I told him I'd think about it."

"You're crazy, Laura."

"No, scared. I'm frightened to death of being alone with him. I . . . I'm afraid I've gotten you into something but I figure it's your fault for engineering all this. I told Craig I'd go if you would come along, too."

"Now I know you're crazy. What'd he say?"

She turned bright red. "He laughed his fool head off."

"I can't say I blame him. A chaperone . . . an out and out chaperone. That's what you're trying to make me."

"But you'll do it won't you?"

Nan shook her head in disbelief. "I suppose so, if that's the only way to get you two together."

"Well . . . you could invite someone. Maybe that nice Mr.

Easton would enjoy coming along."

"Absolutely not. Robert Easton is . . . well it's definitely not one of your better ideas."

"But you'll come anyway?"

"Sure, why not? As long as we don't go to the King Midas."

But they did. Either Craig didn't get the message or he chose to ignore it, and the limousine, with Craig and Laura sitting at a considerable distance from each other, was already turning into the parking area for the expensive club before Nan realized where they were going. She was totally unsettled but kept it to herself rather than make a scene.

Laura enjoyed a limited amount of gambling. The slot machines were her thing. While they waited for their table to be ready they went into the casino to see where the action was. It was at the craps table and Lance was at the center of it. There was a rule against employees gambling but he always managed to get around it.

Nan tried to stay in the background. She glanced at her watch. He was due to start the evening's entertainment in less than ten minutes. By all rights he should have been backstage. He was dressed for it so that was something. But the minutes sped by and he remained at the head of the table, his eyes feverish and glazed as he shook the dice then rolled them with a flourish.

"Come on baby, gimme a ten."

Ten it was. A small crowd had gathered; they sighed their relief and Nan heard someone say that he had built a small bet into nearly two thousand dollars. A short blond woman stood at his elbow. He reached around and kissed her full on the mouth, then handed her the dice.

"Do it to 'em, baby. Bring me some luck."

She kissed the dice and handed them back, clinging to his arm in a possessive way. He rolled again and won.

The dealer looked at his watch. "Come on, Lance. It's show time. Better collect your chips."

"Like hell. They can take the show and stuff it. I'm hot. I can't quit now. Morey can stand in."

Nan stilled an urge to intervene. She couldn't bear to watch. It was a blessing when Craig took her by the arm.

"I didn't know you were a craps addict. That's our table. Didn't you hear the page?"

Nan shook her head. "Sorry. I hope I didn't keep you waiting."

Lance never made it to the show. Morey stood in for him and Nan learned later that Lance had dropped over five hundred after losing everything he had gained.

The evening could have been a total loss except for the successful reunion between Laura and Craig. After their initial shyness, they began to talk about the intervening years and in no time they were laughing and touching. Nan was amused at Craig's obvious inability to keep his hands away from Laura. He was forever patting her hand or arm. She was as starry-eyed as a school girl at her first dance. About ten o'clock Nan cornered Laura in the ladies' room.

"I think I have a headache coming on. Would you mind terribly if I deserted the two of you?"

Laura looked concerned. "Of course not. I'll ask Craig to send you home in the limo . . . unless you want me to go with you," she said somewhat reluctantly.

Nan grinned. "I think I can make it by myself. William and I are old friends."

It came as no surprise to Nan that Craig wasn't overly disappointed by her wish to make an early night of it. He ordered his car brought around, and within a half-hour Nan was on her way home. She felt almost motherly toward the two of them. And like a mother, she worried a little that she had done the right thing in bringing them together. But it was done . . . and there was nothing to do but wait.

As the limousine turned into her street they passed a silver-gray sports car which was parked along the opposite curb a few houses before hers. She caught only a fleeting glimpse but she was sure that it was Robert seated behind the wheel.

As soon as William closed the door behind her she thanked him and told him goodnight. He offered to wait until she was inside but she told him it was unnecessary. A short time later her doorbell chimed.

Nan knew beyond a shadow of a doubt that it was Robert. The question was, why was he here? She stood with her hand against the wall, waiting for her heart to stop its ridiculous pounding. Would he never stop catching her unaware. Just when she thought she could guess his next move he managed to take her by surprise. Well, if he thought she was going to fall all over him just because he came by to ask her out again...he could jolly well forget it. She'd had it where he was concerned. She wasn't about to get involved in another shattering romance. She believed that for all of ten seconds, then almost ran to open the door.

Chapter Eleven

"HELLO, NAN."

"Robert." She stood at the door neither inviting him in nor in any way attempting to make him feel welcome. She had to know what he had in mind before she gave any indication that she was overjoyed to see him.

He shifted from one foot to the other like a little boy caught throwing a ball through a window. "May I come in? There's something I have to tell you."

She hesitated, then moved aside and motioned for him to come in. "We'll sit in the living room."

He raised an eyebrow and she saw him look around as if expecting to see someone hiding in another room. He knew she rarely used the living room, but the way things had gone between them she felt as if she needed the distance which the formal aspect of the living room could provide. He selected a comfortable club chair, and she sat some distance away on a straight-back Empire chair. Any other time he would have made an amused comment but for once he was on his good behavior.

He seemed to have trouble getting started. Nan went to his aid. "Whatever it is you wanted to tell me must be very important to have brought you all the way out here tonight."

"It was . . . it is. I didn't want you to find this out from someone else. I wanted to tell you myself."

Oh, God, she thought, *he's getting married.* But immediately after the thought occurred she realized that there would have been no reason for him to tell her about it. There was a hollow spot in the middle of her stomach. "I really wish you'd tell me. All sorts of terrible pictures are going through my head."

He cleared his throat. "Sorry. I just didn't know how you'd take it. The thing is . . . I had to have your ex-husband fired tonight."

"Lance?" she said stupidly.

"I'm sorry, Nan. I know you and he will be convinced I did it out of anger for having found him in your bed that night, but so help me, that had nothing to do with it."

She carefully folded her hands in her lap. "Do you want to tell me what happened? Although I think I can guess. I was at the club tonight and saw him at the craps table."

"He's in way over his head, Nan. I should never have let it go this far, but when the manager told me he was going to cut off Lance's credit I was afraid you'd think I did it for spite." He ran his fingers through his hair and swore softly. "Three nights in a row he hasn't shown up to emcee the show. The manager couldn't carry him anymore . . . not when the reason is so obvious. I . . . I'm sorry. I know how you must feel."

He looked absolutely wretched as he spoke. Nan wanted to take him in her arms and put his head on her shoulder. Instead, she concentrated on keeping her voice steady. "I appreciate your telling me. You're right, of course, it would have hurt more coming from someone else. It's all over between Lance and me, but I'm still concerned about him." She sighed. "How did he take it?"

"Not very well, so I'm told. He was pretty belligerent, I guess."

"Will he be blacklisted?"

Robert shrugged. "Not officially—but word gets around fast. He'll find it hard to get another job in this business unless he goes to Vegas. He might have a chance there."

Nan shook her head. "It won't matter. He'll just do the same thing all over again."

"Look...I'm sorry to lay all this on you. I know that it doesn't directly pertain to you."

"No...I really appreciate it. Maybe I can figure out a way to handle him if he shows up on my doorstep."

"It won't do any good to sympathize with him...but I guess you know that."

She nodded. "But what's left? I can't give him money; he'd gamble it away. He won't listen to advice. Lord, I thought it was an impossible situation when he was just racing cars. This is even worse."

"I wish I could help."

The last thing she wanted from Robert was his sympathy. She straightened. "Thank you, but there's nothing anyone can do. He'll have to work it out for himself." She rose as if to change the subject. "Can I get you something to drink?"

"Are you having something?"

"I...I don't think so. I had dinner not long ago and I couldn't handle anything else, but I'll be glad to get you something."

He hesitated then stood, shoving his hand into his pockets as if trying to make up his mind. "No...I guess maybe it's a good idea if I leave now."

The emptiness gnawed at Nan's insides. So that *was* the only reason he had come out to see her. She'd hoped that maybe he wanted to try to work things out. She stood and walked with him to the entryway. Once outside, he turned with his hand on the door.

"Oh...by the way. There's something I wanted to give to you." He fished in his pocket and brought out a small parcel. "It's nothing, so don't be disappointed. It's your bracelet. I just had it repaired."

She nodded. "Thank you. That was thoughtful of you."

He shrugged. "Well, I guess I'd better be going."

She watched as he went down the walk and got into his car. "Darn," she said aloud. "If I hadn't been so stupid I could have found *some* way to keep him here a little longer."

It was an hour later as she was reading in bed, when Nan remembered the package and opened it. The bracelet had been repaired but there was something else. In addition to the charms which she had collected over a period of years, there was a new one, a sterling silver jester with movable arms and head and a tinkling bell on the top of his peaked clown's cap. Nan shook it up and down, delighted with the way it appeared to dance. As she rubbed her thumb across the box on which it was standing, the front flipped open to reveal a tiny inscription. She held it to the light. It was a telephone number, Robert's, she guessed, not the same number she had used the night she had tried to find him, but probably his own private number.

Should she call him? She lay back on the pillow and considered the alternatives. Liberated was one thing, but aggressive was another. She wanted him to do the calling. If he had really wanted to see her tonight, he would have stayed. Still . . . he seemed genuinely ill at ease. Had she made him feel less than welcome? Before she could change her mind, she grabbed the phone and dialed. He answered immediately.

"What took you so long?" he asked before he said hello.

"Robert? This is Nan."

"I know. I've been waiting over an hour for your call."

"You couldn't have. You were here less than an hour ago."

"It seems like two hours."

"How did you know I'd call?"

"I knew."

She laughed shakily. "I called to thank you for the jester. He's darling."

"You missed the significance. Either that or you're too polite to say so."

"I don't follow you."

"The jester is also called a fool . . . that's what I've been these past few days. I was a fool to behave the way I did when we walked in and found Lance in your bed. I'm sorry, Nan. I'd like very much to start all over with you. Maybe this time I can get it right." He hesitated and when she didn't answer, his voice came back low and intense. "Look, Nan. I know how you must feel. I was an idiot, I admit it, but damn it, I was jealous. Every time I think of him with you I can feel this anger start to build inside me. I want to be the only man in your life."

A quick vision of him dancing with his cool blonde flashed across her eyes. She swallowed. "Just what did you have in mind, a harem? You seemed to be quite content with your dancing partner the other night."

He laughed. "Good, you're jealous, too. I swear I've seen the last of her. She was simply a stopgap measure. I thought that by seeing her I'd be able to get you out of my mind. But it didn't work. I don't want to see anyone but you."

She tried to laugh but it sounded tinny to her ears. "I do believe you're asking me to go steady, Robert. I didn't know people did that anymore."

He echoed her laugh. "I like the idea. How about you?"

"I . . . I like it very much."

"Incredible! How about if I come back out there tonight?"

"Now?" She knew what he meant but she needed time to think.

"Of course, now. What do you say?"

"I don't think it's a good idea." She ran a quick tongue across her lips. "There's something you ought to understand before we go any farther, Robert. Just because we've decided to see each other exclusively for a while, doesn't mean that I will let you . . . make love to me."

She could almost see his mustache lift at the corners.

"Look, Nan. I'm not going to promise to stop trying, but I swear I'll never persuade you to do anything you don't want to do. I told you, I like to take things slow and easy, make all the stops along the way as we used to say. Okay?"

"Okay. You aren't angry about tonight?"

"Of course not. Although a telephone conversation is a poor way of celebrating our first official commitment to each other. We at least ought to have shared a glass of champagne."

"I'll take a rain check."

"How about tomorrow afternoon?"

"I have to work. I have the morning free, though."

"I can't make it. There's a board meeting at nine-thirty. Heaven only knows how long it will last. Tomorrow night?"

"Fine. Could we make it about eight?"

"Sure. Let's take the tram up to Heavenly Valley for dinner."

"I'd love to. I haven't done that for a couple of years."

"I hate to wait that long to see you. God, I *am* a fool for not settling all this while I was at your house tonight."

Nan looked over at the empty bed. "Maybe it was better this way. I'm glad we worked it out, Robert."

"Me too, Nan. Me too."

After they said goodnight it took Nan a long time to fall asleep, but once she did, her dreams were so erotic that she found it difficult to let them go when the alarm clock buzzed. It was one of the few mornings she could have slept in, but she was so filled to the brim with happiness that it was impossible to remain still. After she had cleared away the remains of her breakfast she went into the backyard and picked an armful of marguerite daisies, circled them with leather ferns, and arranged them in a basket to take to the cemetery. It had been a month since she had visited her parents' graves and she wanted to go, not out of a sense of duty, but from a need to share her happiness with them. She laughed at her own childishness. It wasn't as if she thought they were really there waiting to see her, but it was as close as she could be and she needed that feeling of closeness.

The air was still as she drove down the quiet lane; the cemetery was deserted. She put the flowers next to the headstone and steadied them as she knelt to pull a few weeds which had encroached on the low mounds.

Nan sat back on her heels and compared the names etched in granite. Her father's name was darkened with age but her mother's had yet to succumb to the elements. Her bracelet jingled, reminding her of Robert. She touched the charms, one by one, reliving each landmark occasion; the crossed skis her father had given her the day she graduated from the bunny slopes, the big number one they had given her when she made the dean's list at college, the tennis racket which acknowledged the tournament she had won six years ago at the club, the rose in remembrance of her twenty-first birthday.

There were others but she passed over them and went to the jester.

Her mother had never wanted her to go out with Robert. What would she think now if she knew how things had turned out? Unbidden, her mother's warning repeated itself from out of the past. "Don't ask for trouble, Nan. He's out of your class. Dating him will only break your heart."

Nan stood up. She didn't want to remember what had gone before. He had said it last night. He wanted a chance to start over fresh without the mistakes of the past. Well, that's what she wanted too. One had to take a chance sometimes. She'd never forgive herself if she gave up on Robert without a fair try. She sighed. Usually her visits to the cemetery left her at peace with the world, but today was different. Fortunately, there was too much left to do to have time to worry about it.

Her phone was ringing when she got home. It was Laura. "How's your headache?"

Nan was puzzled. "Headache? I don't follow you."

"The one that so conveniently came up just after dinner last night."

"Oh, that one." Nan grinned. "How'd it go after I left?"

"Just as if the last ten years had never happened. No, that's not true. It was never this good ten years ago. We were just kids then, too young to appreciate what we had."

"Sounds serious."

"It is, at least for me."

"And Craig?"

"I think he feels the same as I do."

"Can you trust him?"

"Yes. That was always his trouble, he was too honest with me."

"What now?"

"I don't know, Nan. I'm just going to cherish each day for what it brings and the devil with the rest of it. Lord, I'd forgotten what it's like to have a man love me." When Nan didn't say anything she added, "I don't mean *make love to me*, I mean love me as if nothing else in the world mattered."

Nan's voice felt stiff in her throat. "I'm glad it turned out so well, Laura. You deserve to be happy." She took a deep breath. "Are you going out to the set today?"

"No. I have too much work to do. Craig's here now but he's in the other room getting ready to leave. I just wanted to call to thank you for everything."

"My pleasure. I hope it works out the way you want it to. Look, I hate to cut you off but I have to get ready for work, too. Thanks for calling."

Nan squeezed her eyes shut. She felt so responsible now that the two of them were back together. Would it last? And what would it do to Laura if Craig were just making time with her until he returned to Los Angeles? She was afraid to think of it. Better to concentrate on the positive side. In all the time since she had known her, Laura had never sounded so happy. That in itself was surely worth something.

If Laura were happy, Cassie Rinella was the exact opposite. It was evident from the moment she arrived on the set that Craig had confronted her with the fact that he was aware of her duplicity. In her temper she lashed out at everyone, Nan included. "It's all your fault. Why couldn't you leave us alone? You had to bring her up here and get things started all over again."

Nan ignored her. Nothing she could have said at this point would have helped. But Cassie wasn't used to being ignored. She grabbed Nan by the shoulder. "You look at me when I'm talking to you."

Nan turned and spoke softly. "Please, Cassie. This isn't helping anything. You're just making yourself look foolish."

"Don't you try to boss me around. You don't run this show just because some windbag of an owner put it in the contract that you had to be here. You're nothing. Do you understand? Nothing!"

She picked up an antique vase and would have thrown it but Craig walked in at that moment.

"Put it down, Cassie," he said quietly.

She looked at him, tears filling her eyes, then slowly put it down and ran from the room.

"Will she be all right?" Nan asked.

"Sure. It'll take a while to adjust, but she knew the score from the beginning. If she hadn't been the one to come between Laura and me I'd feel a little more sympathetic. Cassie makes her own rules and it isn't often that she's called to answer for her actions. This just might be a first." He picked up the vase and replaced it in its proper place.

The split between Craig and Cassie left the rest of the crew

with a rather subdued attitude. Although there was no love lost
between them and Cassie, the simple fact that she had been
around so long had given them a feeling of permanence and
solidity in a profession where one never knew, from one day
to the next, who was in and who was out. Craig evidently
realized this and tempered his criticism to a marked degree.
Cassie did not return to the set that afternoon.

As for Craig himself, he was obviously hard put to keep
from dancing. Several times when he chanced to catch Nan's
eye he winked broadly to let her know that he was on top of
the world. He was irrepressible and, despite her somewhat
negative attitude toward the show business crowd, she really
liked the man.

It was late in the afternoon during a set change when Nan
finally got to talk to him about Laura. She let him bring up the
subject.

He put his hands on her shoulders and looked her straight
in the eyes. "Nan, honey. We owe this all to you. Laura Lee
and I can never repay you for bringing us back together. What
would you like? A part in my next movie, maybe?"

Nan giggled. "Don't be silly. Your career would go right
down the drain. Seriously, though. All I want is for you to
make Laura happy. She loves you very much and I don't want
to see her hurt."

"I'll do my best to see that she isn't. I'd do anything for
that gal."

Nan squeezed his hands. "I know you mean that. I want you
to be happy, too."

"Thanks. That means a lot." The signal came from the set
director that they were ready to go, and the actors took their
places.

The rest of the day was routine. Nan was relieved when
Craig gave the order to wrap it up with a call for seven the
next morning. This time she would make it home in plenty of
time to dress for her date with Robert.

She was beginning to feel a little nervous about going out
with him. Each of their previous dates had come to a traumatic
ending, but surely they knew each other well enough now to
take any misunderstanding in stride. At least that was what she
kept trying to tell herself.

By the time his car pulled into the drive Nan was dressed in her favorite street-length dress of misty-blue crepe de Chine. An ivory sweater knitted in a shell design was enough to ward off the slight chill after the sun went down, and she added the charm bracelet last of all.

Robert, in a brown sports coat, matching checked pants and an ivory silk shirt, looked relaxed and rested when he saw her.

"You look terrific, Nan. Blue must be your best color."

She laughed. "Well, it's a good step above pink with my red hair."

"Bronze, not red. It's too dark to be red."

"Whatever you say. Would you like to sit down for a while or are you ready to go?"

"Let's leave now so that we'll have time to walk around and enjoy the view after we get to the top."

"Sounds great. I thought you might want to, so I wore my low heels."

He took her hand as they walked outside. "You know what they say about great minds."

"Sure. They're guilty of judicious imitation."

He grinned. "I think we lost something in the translation. How about this one. 'A mind grows narrow in proportion as...'"

She flipped her hair over her shoulders and looked up at him. "'As...as the woman puts on a small hat.'"

"God, that's awful, Nan."

"Your turn. How about 'A penny saved is a penny...'"

"'That's worth only a tenth as much in two weeks.'"

She wrinkled her nose. "Too easy. Try this one. 'All work and no play makes Jack...'"

"'A millionaire before he's thirty.'" He gave her a playful shove then closed the car door and went around to the other side. When he sat down next to her, he reached over and picked up her hand, pressing it between his two palms.

"I want you to know, Nan, I'm not taking this lightly. I haven't had a 'steady girl' since my freshman year in college."

She looked up at him, uncertain how to respond. But there was no need. He cupped her chin in his hand and kissed her lightly on the mouth.

Chapter Twelve

ROBERT'S KISS HAD left a special glow which lasted until they joined the people entering the tram to be lifted to the top of the Heavenly Valley run. Compared to the wintertime crowd the number of riders was fairly small, but the holiday mood was clearly in evidence. Some of the passengers were making the trip to enjoy the view, but most of them were planning to have dinner at The Top of the Tram restaurant.

Robert seemed unwilling to let go of Nan's hand even while they were seated on the bench which ran along one side of the tram. As he laced fingers with hers she was aware of the strength in his hands as well as the gentleness which was more vividly apparent. It was a source of wonder to Nan that he chose to be with her. This man could have any woman he wanted, if not because of his bank account, then surely because of his physical attractiveness and his innate courtesy.

He looked down at her. "What are you thinking about? You look like you're a million miles away."

She wasn't about to tell him. She smiled. "It's the mountain. It always does this to me. It's overwhelming."

They felt the jerk as the tram slid over the tower supports. The tourists among them gasped in fear then grinned in delight as they noticed that the locals took it in stride.

He gazed out over the expanse of the lake reflecting the clear blue sky and the backdrop of mountains. "I know what you mean. There is something about the immensity of it all that reduces man to insignificance."

She nodded. "When I'm really feeling down about something I can come up here, or go out on the lake, and realize how unimportant my worries are. It really helps one keep the proper perspective."

"You can see Emerald Bay from here. It has to be one of the most beautiful spots on Earth."

"Um. I think the same thing every time I drive by it. It's even more beautiful from the water."

"Let's take the boat over there this weekend."

She grinned. "Yours or mine?"

He leaned close, staring into her eyes, and for a moment she thought he would kiss her in front of everyone, but he laughed.

"Scared you, didn't I? That's what you get for making glib remarks. We'll take the cruiser. That way I can insist that you do the cooking since I have to steer."

"Great. I'll bring all the food. Do you have any special requests?"

"Anything but liver or smoked oysters."

"You're living dangerously. For all you know I might have very exotic tastes. For example I might decide to serve rattlesnake steak or sow's ear pie."

He grinned. "If you eat it first I'm game to taste it."

"I might do it just to see the expression on your face, so don't tempt me."

He gazed steadily at her for a breathless minute, his eyes dark with an appetite beyond that for food. "Tempt you? My dear, I hope that I already have."

Nan didn't bother to respond. She knew that the answer was shining from her eyes.

They had dinner in the elegantly rustic restaurant where they

were seated by a wall of windows which overlooked the panorama of towns, lake, and mountains spread out below. Lights
had begun to flick on all over the valley and it was like watching
a diorama in a museum become activated after one pushes the
button. All that was missing was the recorded guided tour.

Nan was perfectly at ease, content to sit across the table and
know that for the moment, at least, she belonged to Robert.
His fame had preceded him, but unlike the wild homage paid
to Craig Martindale and his entourage when they appeared in
public, Robert was greeted with respect and a certain degree
of awe. He in turn was gracious, expecting the best but not
overdemanding where service was concerned.

They dawdled over their food as if they were afraid that to
finish was an indication that the evening was drawing to a
close. It was well after ten when they finally left the restaurant.
A young couple were the only other passengers on the trip
down in the tram. Robert nudged Nan. "There's something to
be said about youth and young love. It doesn't know the meaning of inhibitions."

Nan knew what he meant but refused to look in that direction. From the moment they boarded the tram, the pair had
been locked in each other's arms. Robert grinned and put his
arm across the back of the bench behind Nan, his fingers strok-
ing her shoulder. "We aren't that much older than they are,
you know."

Nan met his gaze. "But we ought to set a good example,
don't you think?" she said teasingly.

"As far as I'm concerned they're strictly on their own. We're
not their parents. Besides, maybe it's a good thing for them
to realize that old fogeys like us can be in love, too. Wouldn't
you agree?"

Nan laughed and soon forgot about the other couple. She
was lost in the wonder of being carried across the valley through
the beauty of the star-filled night. When Robert finally took
his arm away it occurred to her that she hadn't needed the tram,
she could have flown without it.

They stopped in town afterward and walked around for a
while. Neither of them wanted to go to a club. Robert had
suggested they go for a drive along the lake and park to watch
the moon but Nan knew where that would lead. It had been

perfect so far. She knew her own weakness and she wasn't about to tempt fate, not yet anyway. It was around eleven when he pulled into the drive at her house. He stood by the door and looked down at her.

"Will you invite me in . . . for a cup of coffee . . . or something?"

"Coffee sounds fine. You know where the kitchen is. I'll just put my sweater away."

When she came in he was already heating water. "I hope you don't mind if I make myself at home," he said. "I miss having a big, roomy kitchen."

"Please do." She finished preparing the coffee and got out mugs from the cupboard. "You have a suite at the King Midas, don't you?"

"Yes. That's where I live most of the time. It's convenient, and there's a kitchen of sorts but it's hardly bigger than the galley on the boat. I keep thinking I'll move back into my house, but it would be foolish for one person to rattle around in a place like that."

"Are you talking about the lodge?"

"No. I mean the place up at the North Shore."

Nan laughed. "Talk about the proverbial scorecard. I suppose I should feel sorry about your having to make such difficult decisions, like which house you should live in, or whether to drive one of your cars or take the limousine to work, but somehow I just can't seem to muster the sympathy."

He grinned and grabbed her wrist. "Okay, that's one for you—but I don't take lightly to being teased, so be warned."

"And I don't take lightly to warnings."

He waited for her to go on but she refused with her eyes. He put his hands on her shoulders. "You didn't finish. You were going to say, 'So what are you going to do about it?' weren't you?"

She waited again and he pulled her against him until her eyes opened wide in expectation.

His voice was husky. "Weren't you, Nan?"

She shook her head.

"The hell you weren't. I can read your mind." He bent and kissed her thoroughly and competently until she was left breathless. Fortunately they were interrupted by the whistle of the tea kettle. Nan pulled away with a little laugh, grateful for the fact that he had been joking when he said that he could read her mind. If it weren't a joke, she was in big trouble.

As if by unspoken agreement, they managed to keep things light until Robert was ready to leave. The intimacy of their isolation could have led to a serious involvement if they had permitted themselves to court danger, but, somehow, knowing the danger was just a kiss away added to the intensity of their need.

At the door Robert reached for her one more time. Their kiss was friendly and chaste.

Nan looked up at him in surprise and he rubbed his nose against her forehead. "Sorry. That's the best I can do if you hope to get rid of me tonight. May I see you tomorrow night?"

"Of course. Shall I cook dinner for you?"

"Sow's ear pie?"

"Nothing quite so exotic, but if you behave yourself I'll take you for a ride in my boat."

He shook his head. "My spirit is willing but the flesh is . . ."

She giggled. "Bound to get wrinkles if it stays out in the sun too long." He made a face but she continued. "Well . . . I guess I can always throw you overboard."

"I'd like to see you try."

She reached up and kissed his cheek. "Goodnight, Robert. Thank you for a perfect evening."

She was almost glad when the door closed behind him. For once they had managed to get through a date without a traumatic scene. They must be making progress.

The situation at the lodge was still rather tense where Cassie was concerned when Nan reported to work the next day. Craig, in a state of euphoria over his reconciliation with Laura, passed it off as unimportant but Nan wondered if Cassie would let them get off so easily. She had, after all, gone to great lengths to keep them apart ten years ago.

But there was little time to worry about it. Shooting was taking place outside that day. The props crew was in the process of setting up the railroadlike tracks on which the camera would move back and forth. They told her it was to enable them to get a smooth shot without flutter when the camera rolled over the ground. The cast was coming out of the trailer after having been made-up when she took her chair just behind the director's. Craig rarely sat down so she had a clear view. He had an abundance of nervous energy and an insatiable need to know exactly what was going on at every minute.

"Okay, Roy. I want a shot of Freddie sneaking out from behind those bushes. You'll have to get the camera closer to the house so when we pan we won't get the trailer in the background. Can you get in tight enough?"

"Can do." The burly cameraman made a circle with his thumb and index finger.

Ten minutes later they were ready to roll. Freddie had concealed himself in the shrubbery and was just starting his furtive movement toward the front of the house when he stood up straight, hands on hips.

"Look, Craig. How the devil am I supposed to find the shovel when somebody forgot to put it under the bush?"

Craig gave the order to cut. "Cassie! Where the devil is she anyway?"

Someone said they had seen her go into the lodge a few minutes ago. Craig sent a props man to hunt for the shovel while he fumed at the delay. "Damn. I can see holding up a production for a major tragedy, but to lose time over simple carelessness is inexcusable."

The props man came back empty-handed and Craig got red in the face as he yelled in no uncertain terms for Cassie to "get the hell out here."

The cameraman jumped to Cassie's defense. "Hey look man, she's never screwed up before. Give her a break."

Nan was uneasy. "Would it help if I go find her?"

Craig looked grim. "It sure couldn't hurt."

As she started toward the front door, a girl yelled and pointed toward a window. "Look, there's smoke all over the place."

The cameraman was the first to move. "My God. Cassie could be in there."

The crew surged toward the entrance, not only to save Cassie, if need be, but to save the lodge. There were still several interior shots to be taken. If anything happened to the lodge they would have to start all over. Craig took complete charge.

"Dwight, you get the fire department; Stan, the fire extinguishers are in the trailer; Bob, you help him." He motioned to the cameramen. "You guys come with me."

They were already at the door and Nan followed them in. Craig yelled at her to close it behind her to stop the draft.

Smoke coming from the balcony area filled the upper portion of the dome. A slim figure, seen in silhouette through the smoke, was holding a flaming cigarette lighter against the bottom end of a drape. Nan ran to the closet and grabbed the fire extinguisher which hung from a wall bracket. One of the men took it from her and dashed up the stairs while Roy, the burly cameraman, followed close after him. He grabbed the figure from behind and held her firmly against his chest. It was Cassie. Nan had guessed it from the beginning.

In no time they had extinguished the fire, keeping the damage, except for a drapery panel, to a bare minimum. But evidently the psychological damage to Cassie went deeper. She appeared to be in a state of shock, due in part to the burns she had sustained on her hands and arms. A cursory examination of the drape made them realize that she had dumped a bottle of liquor on it to start the fire, but in doing so she had spilled a good portion on her arms, which ignited when she lit her cigarette lighter.

Roy carried Cassie down the steps and outside into the fresh air. Nan realized suddenly that the drapes were not the only torch she had seen that day. Roy was carrying a torch for Cassie, big enough to ignite the entire valley. He had hidden the fact pretty well until now.

Cassie's burns proved to be rather minor, but there was no doubt she needed emergency care.

"We could call an ambulance," Nan said, "but it would be faster if we just took her down in a car."

"Right," Craig agreed. "You'd better come along since you know the way."

Nan nodded and Roy started to gather Cassie in his arms. "I'm coming along," Roy insisted. Fortunately, Craig didn't argue.

While they were getting Cassie situated in the back seat of the limousine, Craig yanked down the drape and threw it into the trunk. He shrugged at Nan's unspoken question.

"We'll have to get a duplicate made today or we won't be able to shoot in sequence tomorrow."

Nan sighed. "That's right, the show must go on."

The closest hospital was at South Lake Tahoe. William drove faster than Nan would have believed possible, but the excessive weight of the huge automobile gave an added measure of safety on the mountainous road. Cassie was in considerable discomfort but Roy seemed even more affected by the pain. Craig, seated in the front seat along with the driver, glanced back several times with a curious expression on his face. Apparently he, too, had been unaware of the cameraman's feelings for Cassie.

Nan felt more than a little apprehensive. Cassie, as a mean, vindictive girlfriend of long standing, was less a threat to Laura's happiness than this unhappy creature who had been driven to arson to keep the man she loved. Also, with Roy in the picture as a new love interest, would Craig begin to feel the first twinges of jealousy? Nan mentally shook herself. She was asking for trouble. She was making the situation sound like a melodrama, a soap opera. But she wanted so much for Laura to be happy.

The limousine swung into the emergency entrance at Barton Memorial Hospital. Once again the name of Craig Martindale worked its magic and red tape was cut like so many spiderwebs by a buzz saw. A cursory examination proved the burns to be minor but Cassie's mental condition made an overnight stay in the hospital mandatory. The doctor told them there was nothing to be gained by their waiting around. Roy planted his big feet firmly in the middle of the waiting-room floor and said that he wouldn't budge an inch until she was resting comfortably.

Surprisingly, Craig accepted it. "Okay, pal. You can pack it in for today. We'll see that your equipment is taken care of and I'll send the limo around for you later this afternoon." He looked at his watch. "In the meantime, I've got to see what we can do to repair the damages so we'll be ready to start shooting inside by tomorrow."

Once back in the limousine, Craig looked at Nan. "You've

every right to be upset about the damage to the lodge. I appreciate your not having a fit over it. A fire, especially one that was deliberately set, was the last thing in the world I would have expected."

"Well, I can't say I'm happy about it, but as far as I could tell, the damage to the wall itself was superficial. The drape is ruined but the material is not all that unusual. I think it can be replaced."

"By tomorrow?"

"No way. This is one time you have to bow to the impossible, Craig. The size is super-long. I would guess at least a hundred twenty inches because of the dome ceiling. That means they have to be custom-made."

He forced a grin. "I'll leave it up to you, Nan. I know you can handle it. Just make sure everything's ready to go by nine A.M."

"Me? That's not part of my job. I'm a real estate agent, remember?"

"And the best there is. Well, second best. And speaking of Laura, why don't I run over and take her to lunch while you scout up someone to do the drape?"

Nan groaned but couldn't keep the smile from her voice. She'd have done anything to keep the fires burning between Craig and Laura. "All right, slave driver. Flattery wins again. But how am I to pay for all this? It's going to be very expensive."

He pulled out his checkbook and scribbled his name. "There. You can fill in the amount, whatever it is. I'll have William drop me off at the realty office and you can keep the car."

"Do you want me to come back for you after I finish . . . if I ever do?"

"No. I'll take a cab."

Laura's car was parked in the lot when they arrived at Pinnacle Realty. Craig's eyes mirrored his pleasure and he grinned broadly as he got out of the car.

"Have fun, sweetie."

Nan resisted the urge to stick her tongue out at him as she settled back against the seat. William looked at her through the rearview mirror.

"Where to, Miss Gilliam?"

She groaned. "I wish I knew. Make a right on Fifty and we'll take it from there."

A sudden inspiration made her reach for her handbag and Robert's office phone number. A short time later she was connected by mobile phone with Robert's secretary who provided Nan with the name of the interior decorator who designed the office décor. As she guessed, it was the same firm that had designed the interior of the lodge. She gave William the address and within the next hour, a trio of women were hard at work on the drape. Thanks to their computerized records, they were even able to come up with the proper measurements for that particular window. Of course, Craig's bank account was considerably lighter, but compared to the cost of keeping a cinematography crew standing by on hold, the price was bound to be minimal.

Nan treated William to a steak and salad at one of the cafeteria-type steak houses on Emerald Bay Road. While they were eating, William suggested that if she wanted to call it a day he would see that her car was brought down from the lodge when the crew came down for the night. She was tempted, knowing that she still had to shop for dinner, but her conscience won out and she made the trip back up the mountain.

There wasn't much going on when she got there. Craig hadn't come back and no one took over the business of directing. Maybe no one had the authority. It was, after all, Craig's picture. She checked out the inside of the lodge and discovered an amorous couple in the hot tub, a pastime which was strictly off limits. Fortunately, the bedrooms were still intact, since most of the crew had taken the occasion to sunbathe or play cards inside one of the trailers.

She had saved the burned area until last. It was going to be hard to explain this to Robert. She hated even thinking about it. Luckily the damage was mostly from smoke. The decorator had told her that the drapes had been treated with fire retardent, a fact which had prevented an immediate flare-up when the flames ignited the alcohol. The wall would have to be scrubbed down, of course, but that would take a half-hour or less. The smoke smell was another thing. Fortunately for the shooting schedule, the camera didn't record smells.

About three o'clock, Craig called to say that he had gone back to the hospital to check on Cassie's condition and wouldn't be back at the lodge for the day. That meant a wrap, so she closed up the lodge and went home.

She would have liked to spend hours over the dinner for Robert but she still had to arrange for a cleaning crew to be at the lodge at seven in the morning. A quick call to the decorator assured her that they were on schedule and would meet her at eight the following morning at the lodge. She shook her head. Incredible what money could do. The last time she had drapes made she was lucky to have them delivered within four weeks.

With time running short she settled on shrimp and scallops for dinner along with french fries cut super thin and a delicious carrot, raisin, and coconut coleslaw. A loaf of honey-wheat bread dough went from the freezer into the warming oven so that it would rise in time to be served hot from the oven. She cut some small zucchini into fat strips and let them marinate in Italian dressing while she cut mushrooms, carrot slivers, green pepper, and cabbage into a casserole dish and dotted them with lemon juice and butter. Then she dumped the zucchini on top and jumbled it all together with a fork. After it was in the oven she ran a tub full of water for her bath. By the time Robert arrived everything was ready.

Ready . . . she smiled as she went to the door. *Boy am I ready*.

Chapter Thirteen

NAN PULLED HER peach-colored knit blouse modestly down over the top of her jeans before she opened the door. Robert, also wearing jeans and sneakers, looked more masculine than ever in a knitted white shirt which emphasized his broad shoulders. His hair, still damp from the shower, curled slightly around his ears despite his habitual effort to smooth it down.

Eyes gleaming with anticipation, hands behind his back, he bent down to kiss her upturned face. "I'll consider that an appetizer."

"Oh really? If you think I'm going to ask what you want for the main course, forget it, buster."

"I'm concentrating my efforts on dessert."

She gave him a look. "You're impossible. What are you hiding behind your back?"

"Roses and forget-me-nots." He handed them to her with a flourish. "For you. The florist assured me they would get the message across."

Nan took them and held them to her face. "He's right. They did. They're just lovely. Thank you, Robert."

"I hope you like yellow roses. I knew they'd match your dishes."

"Perfect. I didn't think men noticed things like that."

"Female chauvinist! What do you think we are, sex objects without any real sensitivity?"

She laughed. "All right, Robert. That's enough from you. You're taking a chance acting so smart before you get fed."

"Are you threatening me?"

"Sure, why not?"

"No reason. I just wondered."

She linked her hand with his and led him out to the deck. "We have a few minutes before the bread is due to go into the oven. I want to talk to you."

"Oh? Sounds serious."

"It is. We had some problems up at the lodge today. One of the crew set fire to a drape in the main room. It didn't flare up to any extent, but one of the drapes was ruined and the wall will have to be cleaned. I wanted you to know about it right away." She wrinkled her nose. "Maybe I should have saved it until after dinner."

"Was anyone hurt?"

"Not seriously. Cassie Rinella is staying overnight in the hospital but more for her emotional problems than because of her burns. I've already arranged to have the drape replaced by morning, right after the cleaning crew scrubs down the wall. I got the name of your decorator from Mrs. Mansfield."

She watched his face to judge his reaction. He nodded as if the computer in his head were carefully tabulating each comment, then fastened her with his gaze. "Isn't it time to put the bread in the oven?"

She smiled and pulled his face down to hers then found his lips. "Thank you," she murmured against his mouth. "Thank you for not saying 'I told you so.' I wanted so much for nothing to be damaged while they rented the lodge."

As he swept her into his arms it occurred to her that the real damage was being done to her heart. She managed to stop things before they went too far by remembering the bread which was fast rising over the edge of the pan.

They finished preparing the food together, then ate leisurely, spending more time looking at each other than at their dinner. Afterward, Nan stacked the dishes in the sink over Robert's protest that they wash and dry them.

"Don't be silly," she said. "I'll put them all in the dishwasher after you leave. I think you're just trying to get out of going for a ride in my boat."

"Not a chance. Do I get to row?"

"If you play your cards right." She reached up and squeezed his rather obvious biceps. "You certainly need to do something to build a little muscle."

He shook his head. "Oh, little girl, you do love to live dangerously. One of these days I'll forget myself and make you pay for every single one of your little barbs."

She ran out the back door and down toward the pier. Hearing the door slam behind him she turned and waggled her fingers at him. "Promises, promises!"

The lake was like glass—a dark mirror reflecting the onset of night against a fringe of soft puffy clouds. Along the south shore a necklace of lights flickered red, green, blue, and yellow in the occasional wake of a passing boat. Nan tucked her legs underneath the low seat.

"I should have brought the fishing poles. Do you like to fish?"

"Love it. Are you any good?"

She looked at him to see if it were a loaded question and decided it wasn't. "I haven't had much experience but I enjoy it just the same."

A muscle moved along the side of his jaw and she caught her breath. *Damn! I didn't mean it to come out that way.* Her voice was dry. "Okay, smarty. No matter what I said, you would have taken it the wrong way."

He tried to look innocent but didn't quite succeed. "Oh? What do you mean?"

"Forget it. Keep your mind on rowing the boat."

He grinned. "I thought you said you had a ten-horse motor."

"I do. But this keeps your hands busy."

He looked at her and rested the oars, then, slowly rising to a standing position with his gaze still on her face, he reached out to her. "Look, Ma. No hands."

"Robert, sit down for pete's sake. You're going to tip the boat over."

"Then make room for me."

"I can't. It's too narrow."

"You'd better because here I come."

With the boat shifting dangerously from side to side, he made his way over to where she was sitting. Out of desperation Nan slid to one side, grateful that the boat was still afloat. He put his arm around her.

"There. Isn't that better?"

She leaned her head against his shoulder. "Infinitely. But I still think you're crazy."

"Mmm." He nuzzled her neck below her ear. "Still think so?"

"I don't know. Do it again."

"Like this, and this . . . and this?"

She pulled away. "Nope. You've proved your point." She laughed shakily. "Maybe we'd better return to a captain-and-crew status. We're starting to rock the boat in more ways than one."

"We wouldn't if you didn't make waves." He held onto the side of the boat with his left hand and looked around. "Not that I'm being critical, but a rowboat does have its limitations."

"Uh-huh. Sort of a built in chaperone, wouldn't you say?"

"I couldn't have put it better. Next time we'll take the cruiser."

"And a chaperone?"

"Not on your life."

"I'll have to remember that."

He grinned. "Don't worry. I'm not going to let you forget it."

After a while they each took an oar and managed, with only a few minor mishaps, to get the boat back to the pier. When they had it securely tied Robert took her hand and walked her across the grass.

She reached for his other hand as they entered the house. "Would you like some coffee or something to drink?"

"I don't think so. Let's turn on the stereo and listen to some music."

"Good idea. What kind do you like?"

"Something soft and romantic, mood music."

She put on a recording of theme music from motion pictures. "I hope you like Mantovani. He's one of my favorites."

"I like whatever you like."

"Oh?" She eyed him quizzically. "Then you must be wild about German chocolate cake and raw cabbage and cashmere sweaters."

"Absolutely."

"And cold dill pickles and folded potato chips and dandelion fuzz."

"Couldn't live without them."

"And children."

He looked up slowly, his eyes locking with hers as he pulled her close. Their gaze held for what seemed like ages, then he reached up and cupped her chin in the palm of his hand. "Children? Yes. I'd like children. As long as they looked like you."

Nan was suddenly, unexplainably afraid. For some silly reason tears burned at the back of her eyelids and she was terrified that they would spill over. She pulled away.

"Sorry. I didn't mean to say that. I think it might be a good idea if we had some coffee after all." She made a bee-line for the kitchen, drying her eyes quickly before he followed after her.

As if sensing her change in mood, he wisely refrained from pursuing the subject, nor did he comment about her damp eyelashes. That, in itself, endeared him to her.

They spent the rest of the evening in casual conversation. It was as if neither of them dared trespass beyond unspoken barriers in their conversation. Nan's remark about children had sobered them and they both seemed to want to think about it before they even remotely touched on the subject again.

When he said goodnight at the door, Robert held her close and kissed her with subdued passion. He made no clever remarks about staying the night, nor did he attempt any familiarity. Nan had mixed emotions. She was glad that she didn't have to put him off, but on the other hand...

Closing the door behind him she sighed and went to the kitchen. It had been some day! Dear heaven! Why had she made that stupid remark? She must have been out of her mind. It was almost as if she were hinting, none to subtly, about marriage. She felt her face flame. Well...he didn't appear angry. Tomorrow night would tell. If he seemed cool and unapproachable it would be a good bet that the remark had bothered him. She glanced at the phone. Maybe he'd call her after he got home. She hurried through the work in the kitchen then took a quick shower with the phone readily available just outside the shower door. But he didn't call. Not until the following afternoon while she was up at the lodge.

Nan had gone up to the lodge shortly after six-thirty the next morning to make certain she arrived before the cleaning crew. By seven-thirty they still hadn't gotten there and she was becoming frantic. The decorator was due to hang the drape in less than a half-hour. She was on her way to the telephone when the truck rounded the bend in the lane and swung into the parking area. Breathing a prayer of gratitude, she ran out to meet them.

"You're really going to have to hurry to finish in time. Bring your ladder because some of the smoke damage is up rather high."

They followed after her with less eagerness than she had hoped, but by the time the cinematography crew started to disperse to their separate assignments, the cleaning men were nearly finished. The decorator was only a half-hour late. Nan detected a slight color variation between the old panels and the new, but it was visible only with careful inspection. The woman from the shop had come out herself to make sure everything was done properly. She was extremely apologetic. "I'm dreadfully sorry but we just ran out of time and were unable to do the bottom hem. Since I knew you had to have them for today, I taped them and pressed it into place. They'll hold, you can count on that, but they aren't done properly."

Nan looked them over. "I think you did a fine job. As to the hem, we can do that later. The important thing is not to hold up the shooting schedule." She thanked the two women and finally managed to get rid of them before the set crew came in.

Craig was not surprised to see everything cleaned and in its proper place. He was used to having his way. But nevertheless, he was pleased with Nan's efforts and let her know it.

"Did you see the morning headlines?" he asked.

She shook her head. "I just threw the paper into the house." She frowned. "Oh dear. I hope they didn't write up the story about the fire."

"You kidding? I'd have sued them if they didn't. It took me an hour and twenty-five bucks just to get it written up the way I wanted." He spread a copy of the paper out in front of her. "There it is: 'Jinx Plagues Evil Heritage Set.' This beats any kind of advertising we could have bought and paid for," he said, rubbing his hands together.

Nan skimmed the half-page article which was complete with a photograph of Craig looking worried and frightened as he "read through the shooting script." The text of the article went on to say that strange happenings had taken place all during the filming of the movie both here and on location in the desert. Famed director Craig Martindale had supposedly seriously considered shelving the movie out of regard for his crew's safety, but in the true spirit of the motion picture community, he felt a commitment had been made to the public and they would continue, whatever the risk.

Nan was appalled. "Is that the story you gave them?"

He grinned. "Practically word for word."

"But it isn't true."

He looked at her with impatience. "Well, what should I have told them? That some half-crazy woman tried to burn the place down with everybody in it? Cassie's got enough to answer for without a rap like that hanging over her head. I'll see that she gets the help she needs. She sure as hell wouldn't get it by going to prison." He grinned. "Besides, this is like pure gold at the box office."

Nan shook her head. "You make it sound so sensible that it scares me. I think I've been up here too long. Things like this never happen in the real estate business."

"Don't kid yourself, lady. Haven't you ever heard of planting a big shrub in front of a house to hide the place where the foundation is cracked? Or baking fresh bread in the oven to hide the musty smell from damp and moldy plaster?"

She was saved from having to answer by a message from one of the crew who said she had a telephone call waiting for her in the trailer.

Craig chuckled as she walked away. "Expediency, Nan. That's the name of the game."

She picked up the receiver with more apprehension than she cared to admit, even to herself. "This is Nan Gilliam."

"Yes, Ms. Gilliam. This is Claudia Mansfield, Mr. Easton's private secretary. He asked me to give you a message."

Nan felt her knees go weak and was grateful for the chair placed next to the phone. "Yes, Ms. Mansfield."

"He asked me to relay the information that something important has come up and he will be unable to see you tonight."

"I see." Nan hesitated, wishing she had the nerve to question the woman further.

"Mr. Easton also wished me to tell you that he would call you later."

Nan stiffened her back, hoping to steady her voice. "Thank you for your trouble Mrs. Mansfield."

"Certainly. Goodbye."

Numbly, Nan hung up the phone as she attempted to look normal. The least he could have done was to have made the call himself. It was that unbelievably stupid remark she had made about children. That *had* to be it! He must have felt he was being forced into a corner. Oh God, how could she have been so dumb?

Somehow Nan managed to convey her thanks and get out of the trailer before she made a fool of herself. A few deep breaths of fresh air settled her nerves to a degree before she had to face anyone.

They were all set to start the first take but Roy still had not arrived on location. William had told Craig that the cameraman was going to the hospital to see Cassie before he came to work. Craig was furious and Nan wondered if it were because Roy was going to see Cassie, or because Roy was holding up the shooting schedule. Whatever it was, Craig didn't say, and within fifteen minutes, a cab pulled into the lot and Roy jumped out.

Nan went to meet him. "How's Cassie this morning?"

"A lot better. I'm leaving at noon to take her back to the hotel."

He looked much better himself and Nan wondered if perhaps the two of them had come to an understanding of sorts. Roy wasted no time in getting his equipment set up, and a few minutes later the players were in their places and the order was given to roll the cameras.

Craig didn't complain when Roy told him he would be gone during the lunch hour. They managed to work around him until he returned, then everyone seemed to give the added measure of effort which resulted in an exceptionally fine series of takes for the day.

By the time Nan got home she felt as if she had been gone for a week. She took a hot bath and collapsed on the bed, too mentally and physically exhausted to care about anything but the promised phone call from Robert.

It was after eleven when the phone rang. She dragged herself out of the depths of a nightmare of children brandishing clubs, pursuing Robert down the beach. Her voice was radiant with the expectation of hearing his warm laughter, but it was a wrong number.

She lay back on the bed and stared at the ceiling with its thousands of plaster pebbles sprayed on in an off-white, miniature moonscape. Was there anything worse than waiting for a phone call? She blinked back the tears. Damn! She felt so helpless just lying there waiting. Why couldn't her personal problems be the kind she could work out with logic like those at the real estate office? For example the problem she'd had over her mother's health care.

It wasn't as if she hadn't tried. When the nursing home had informed her that the patients would be moved to the new location Nan and several other families had gone to court in an attempt to prevent the sale of the property to the construction company. But predictably, big business won out over the little people and the patients were transferred to the new building.

She had felt so helpless! The hardest thing she had ever done in her life was to try to help her mother understand why she had to be moved. It had been hopeless from the start. A few days after the move her mother came down with pneumonia and died a short time later.

It had taken Nan a long time to get over it. Fortunately she had her work to keep her busy. Her natural optimism helped her through the rough periods and she felt that her life was interesting and fulfilling. She hadn't really needed anyone... until Robert.

As she started to get up to fix a cup of tea, the phone rang again. In her haste to get to it she tripped over a rug and had to catch herself. "H-hello," she gasped, rubbing her ankle.

"Nan? Are you all right? I was about to give up."

"Robert? Is that you?" She felt as if it were just too good to be true, but it really was him at the other end of the line. His voice was husky.

"Lord, it's good to hear your voice. I had to fly down to San Diego this morning. You got my message?"

"From Ms. Mansfield? Yes. She called me up at the lodge."

"I'm sorry I couldn't phone you myself but there was an unexpected board meeting with one of our companies and I had to be there to bone up on some statistics beforehand."

"I understand." She swallowed. "But I missed you."

"That's the best news I've had all day." She could hear him sigh as if he had just relaxed into a comfortable position. "If I weren't so beat I'd run out to see you." There was a pause as if he were waiting for an answer. Finally he spoke. His voice was low. "Nan... I think it's time we did something about the distance that separates us." She listened, her heart beating too loud for comfort as he continued. "I'm getting tired of saying goodnight over the telephone."

Chapter Fourteen

"WH-WHAT DID you say?" Nan asked.

He laughed. "I said I'm tired of saying goodnight to you over the telephone."

"Oh?"

"'Oh.' Is that all you have to say?"

"I . . . I'm not sure what to say," she said carefully.

"Well, maybe that's a good way to leave it for tonight. This is something that needs to be said in person."

"It . . . sounds serious."

"Right. Dinner tomorrow night?"

"Love to. What time? I have the afternoon off."

"Perfect. How about five? We could take the boat out and have dinner on board. Okay?"

"Fantastic. Your boat or mine?"

He chuckled deep in his throat. "Yours is too small for what I have in mind."

"I assume you're referring to dinner."

"We'll start with that."

They talked for a while about his trip and her day on the set, but Nan was scarcely aware of what they were saying. Her mind was on the earlier things he had said, and exactly what he had meant by them. When they hung up at last, she still was no closer to knowing what he had meant. It wasn't like Robert to be so inscrutable.

Getting up in the morning was much easier when she had something to look forward to, Nan decided as she got ready for work the next day. Since the telephone call from Craig asking her to find a shooting location, her life had become filled with a sense of immediacy and a need to keep on top of things. Pressure, some people would have called it, but she thrived on it. At the same time she realized that she was a private person who needed her time alone. A paradox, perhaps, but she was finding life more interesting, more stimulating than it had been for years.

Who would have thought a few short weeks ago that she would be rubbing shoulders with some of Hollywood's brightest stars? And certainly no one could have convinced her that Robert Easton, whom she had known and hated, the head of a financial conglomerate, would take possession of all her waking thoughts.

She smiled. He missed her. He hated to say goodnight. The feeling was certainly mutual, but where did they go from there? What would she say if he asked her to share his apartment? It went against her feelings of rightness, but if it came to that, could she refuse? She pushed the thought out of her mind. She knew in the end she'd do what she had to do. Marriage to Lance had built up a strength she had thought beyond her capacity.

As she drove to the lodge, Nan admitted to herself that despite her present mood of exhilaration she felt an underlying apprehension. Perhaps it was Lance and his problems or perhaps it was her mother's old warning, that Robert was out of her class, coming back to haunt her. Or perhaps she had never really outgrown her teenage feelings of inadequacy. Did people ever really change? Nan knew quite a number of people who had attained a high degree of success. On the outside they appeared confident to the point of being egotistic, but when one took the time to know them, they were as vulnerable as the next person. She shrugged. The subject was too heavy to ruin such a fine day. She was going out with Robert later in the afternoon. Besides, her mother hadn't *always* been right. The glow settled around her once more and she relaxed against the car seat as she smiled with the anticipation of seeing Robert.

When Nan arrived at the lodge, the crew seemed to be in good spirits. Most of them had the afternoon off and were mulling over plans to visit the casinos, drive around the lake, or just relax and get caught up on their sleep. Craig was flying down to Los Angeles to view the screening of the most recent takes. They had gone through their first editing in one of the trailers, and much of the footage had ended up on the cutting-room floor. What was left, according to Craig, would be two hours of edge-of-the-chair drama that would have made Hitchcock drool with envy.

When she went in to take her chair just off set, Nan was surprised to see Laura sitting quietly, waiting for the shooting to begin. "Laura . . . how nice. I didn't expect to see you here."

Laura looked embarrassed. "I really shouldn't be, either. The work is stacked up to the ceiling back at the office." She shrugged. "But Craig invited me to fly down to L.A. with him and I just couldn't refuse."

"It sounds like you've settled all your differences."

"Not all, but we're trying to put something together after the years we wasted. I don't know if anything will come of it, but we'll see."

Nan studied her face. "I've never seen you looking better, Laura."

She flushed. "You must have been reading Craig's script. He said the same thing. You're both blind, but I love it."

The only bad moments of the morning took place when Cassie Rinella returned to the lodge. There was little trace of the burns, just a slight redness on her arms and on one side of her face. The real change was in her behavior. She was subdued and withdrawn, her eyes flat and lifeless. The only time she seemed to come alive was when Roy put his arm around her. Maybe something would come of that, given time. Roy was certainly protective of her. Nan had worried about what would happen when Cassie came onto the set and saw Laura, but when she did, Cassie's gaze slid right over her as if she were a piece of furniture.

Thankfully, they all got through the morning with a minimum of friction, and by noon Craig had given the order to wrap it up until the 8 A.M. call the next day.

When she finally got home, Nan felt an urgency that she was hard put to describe. She wanted it to be time for Robert. Each minute spent away from him was like an hour on a treadmill. She changed clothes three times then settled on a coral Chinese silk blouse with a white sharkskin skirt deeply pleated in front and flared for comfort. The skirt zipped off to reveal a pair of shorts which would be more suitable for the boat. The coral sandals matched her blouse and would be appropriate for almost anything they might decide to do.

She carried a straw basket purse which was topped with coral and white silk geraniums and daisies. At the last minute she added a large white straw picture hat, partly because she liked hats, and partly to protect her face from the sun. She didn't have freckles anymore, but she knew that staying in the sun for any length of time was simply tempting the fate which controlled redheads.

If she could have found a word to describe Robert when he arrived, it would have meant mischievous anticipation. He was wearing white ducks with a blue knit shirt and a darker blue jacket slung across one shoulder. Dark blue deck shoes squeaked slightly on the slate path to the entranceway as he came into her house.

He grabbed her and spun her around with an abundance of energy. "Lord, what a perfect day. We couldn't have ordered better weather. You look more beautiful every time I see you."

"Be serious. Are you ready to go?"

He held her as if reluctant to let her out of his arms. "Don't rush me. It's been too long since I last saw you, and I want to take an inventory."

She giggled. "Silly. It was the day before yesterday."

He pressed his mouth against her throat, taking it away only to speak. "It seems like a week."

"I know. I missed seeing you last night, but I'm glad you called. You sounded awfully mysterious, though."

"True." He pulled his lower lip up over his mustache in a pensive look. "We'll talk about it later. Right now I think we'd better be leaving before we decide to stay here."

Robert's boat, bearing the Easton emblem, was lying at anchor, fueled and ready to go. The canvas had already been stowed by a marina attendant whom Robert hired to care for the cruiser. A short time later Robert hauled in the lines and eased the throttle into reverse as he negotiated their way into the channel.

"I thought we'd head over toward Emerald Bay and cruise around the island, then continue on up to Sugarpine Point and turn around."

The lake was slightly choppy with a light breeze coming out of the north, an ideal day for the dozens of boats dotting the lake. A group of sailboats appeared to be having a race and Nan was appalled at the chances a couple of them were taking. One in particular heeled over so sharply that she was sure they had lost control, but at the last instant it righted itself and surged ahead.

As the cruiser entered the bay between Emerald Point and Eagle Point, the water became still and they could see trout resting on the bottom nearly a hundred feet down. In areas where the depth went to over a thousand feet, the lake was a rich, cobalt blue, but in the shallower water near the island and the shore, it changed to a vibrant emerald green. Robert slowed the motor to an idle and let the boat drift to a stop just offshore from Vikingsholm Castle.

"What say we drop anchor here and lie in the sun on the deck?"

"Sure."

He looked at her for a few seconds. "Did you bring something more comfortable to wear?"

"Of course." Without hesitation she unzipped her skirt and stepped carefully out of it, then folded it and laid it on the chair. "How's that?"

He grinned. "Don't stop there on my account."

She fastened her gaze on his face. "Well, if you insist." Slowly, she undid her blouse, button by button, beginning at the top and progressing down to the top of her shorts. It might have been her imagination but she could have sworn she saw perspiration bead on his upper lip. Reaching behind her she pulled the tail of her blouse out from the constriction of her shorts. Then, still watching his face, she reached under her blouse and unzipped her shorts. They dropped to the deck and she kicked them aside with her foot. Her blouse came down over her hips and she did a little dance which she thought looked rather seductive but from his grin, decided it must have been funny rather than sexy. With a wide grin, she threw off the blouse and stood facing him in a trim, white, rather sedate, two-piece bathing suit.

"Fooled you, didn't I? That should teach you not to make smart remarks."

He threw his head back and laughed. "Is that what they call 'the layered look'? If so, I approve."

"You'd better, because that's all there is, folks."

He spread a pair of mats on the deck. "Care to take your place in the sun?" She started to sit down but he stopped her. "You'd better take the other one."

"Oh? Why? What's the difference?"

"You said you sleep on the left. I thought you might be more comfortable."

She gave him a look and would have told him that the mats could hardly be considered twin beds, but on second thought decided to skip it. With Robert, it was often better to keep her mouth shut unless she wanted to risk a compromising conversation.

He stretched out on the mat next to hers, seemingly unaware of their closeness. "Would you like me to rub some lotion on your back?" he asked.

There was something in his voice that made her hesitate. She grinned. "No, thank you just the same. If I need it I can dab it on myself."

"Kill-joy. Then how about rubbing some on my back?"

"You're as brown as a beach bum. You need tanning lotion as much as I need freckles."

He stuck out his lower lip in a pout. "Okay, but think how bad you're going to feel when I'm too sore to put on my shirt." He flopped over on his stomach and closed his eyes.

Nan turned on her stomach, propping herself up on her elbows. It was pleasant to lie there and look at him. He was nude to the waist. An elastic-type swim suit snugged against his narrow hips, and above it his back was corded with muscles which moved to the rhythm of his breathing.

There wasn't an ounce of fat on him. He looked muscular and hard from the width of his shoulders down the length of his hairy legs. Against her will, she compared him to Lance. There was a softness about Lance that never disappeared, even during his violently athletic periods when he was soaring on his kite off the cliffs at Baja. His hands, too, were soft and yielding.

Robert stirred, bringing her thoughts back to him, but his eyes remained closed.

Lord, she wanted to touch him. Despite her resolve not to, Nan reached for the bottle of lotion and slowly lifted the hinged top. Still watching him, she emptied a generous amount of lotion into her palm and warmed it in the hollow of her hand. Swinging her legs around she leaned over him until her hair, hanging loose around her shoulders, drifted over him like a veil. Her touch was so light that she was doubtful he had noticed, but she felt him tense.

"You weakened," he said, his voice low and drowsy.

"Um. I couldn't let you burn." She knew it was a lie, and she knew that he knew. It only added to the excitement. Begining at his shoulders, Nan worked the lotion lightly into his skin until he glistened warm and golden in the sun.

"You could make a fortune at this. Your hands are so talented I think I'll insure them."

"You do that."

"All right. I'll take care of that when I change the rest of your insurance over to the family plan."

She stopped, thinking she had missed something. "I . . . I don't follow you."

"Oh, but I want you to . . . for the rest of your life. I was going to save this for tonight when the moonlight's shining on the water and we're drinking a glass of wine, and there's soft music on the radio, but I have no willpower. I want to marry you, Nan. I love you more than I've ever loved anyone in my entire life."

Her hand stopped its progress down his back as she stared

at him lying still and relaxed. Had he actually proposed to her
or was she having a fantasy?

"I think you've been touched by the heat!" She tried to laugh
but the sound came out strangled.

"Why do you say that?"

"Well, because. No man proposes to a woman while he's
lying on his stomach with his eyes closed."

"Why not? I'm afraid if I move you'll stop. So what's your
answer?"

"To what?"

"About marrying me, of course. Will you?"

"Yes."

"Good. A little lower to the right, please."

She smacked him soundly across his bottom. "Forget it,
buster. I've just been proposed to, and I want a little romance."

He stretched like a heat-drugged cat in the sun then rolled
over and sat up. "So it's romance you want." He moved toward
her, a devilish light flickering in his eyes. "Your mat or mine?"

"Robert . . . *Robert!* Now don't get carried away," she
warned.

"It's you who'll get carried away if you don't stop leaning
over like that."

Nan's hands flew to the top of her swimsuit but realized too
late that he was teasing. He reached for her and pulled her into
his arms. He was warm from the sun. The lotion had made his
skin supple and fragrant, dangerously enticing. He kissed her
and she felt the warmth spread through her body. She was
conscious of her near nakedness in the swimsuit, and even
more aware of his skin against hers. He traced a line across
her shoulder with his mouth.

"Did you really mean it? That you would marry me?"

"Are you trying to back out already?"

"Be serious, Nan. I knew a week ago that I wanted to marry
you but I wasn't sure how you'd feel about getting married
again after your experience with Lance. I was so afraid you'd
turn me down before you even gave it a chance."

She stroked the back of his neck with her free hand. "When
I first divorced Lance I thought I'd never dare risk marriage
a second time. I was beginning to think that happy marriages

were not real, but just a big advertising campaign like so much else in the world. Then when I got to know you I realized how desperately I needed you." She pressed her mouth against his shoulder. "It's like a part of me is missing when you're away."

"My feelings exactly. Can we make it soon? I don't think I could handle a long engagement."

"I . . . I don't know. Do you want a large wedding?"

He made a face. "Only if you do. I'm not one for pomp and circumstance, but I'll go along with whatever you want."

"I'd rather it was small. Just a half-dozen or fewer of our close friends. It would be nice if we could hold it in a chapel. There's a small one at the church I attend."

"Sounds perfect to me. We'll need to send out announcements but we can do that after the fact if that's all right. We'll probably need to have a reception later on, but there is no hurry."

She held him off at arm's length and looked closely at him. "Are you really sure this is what you want to do, Robert. We've actually known each other for such a short time. I couldn't bear it if I made another mistake."

"I've never been more sure of anything in my entire life. God, I wish I knew how to tell you the way I feel about you. It's like . . ." He looked at her in dismay. "I don't know. It's as if there is nothing left in the world for me if I don't have you."

"I'm not disputing the physical need. It's pretty obvious we both have our share of those particular feelings, but I have to know that our love goes beyond that."

He shrugged. "I can't give you any guarantees. Life doesn't work that way. But God help me, I'll do everything in my power to make you happy, Nan. We can make a beautiful marriage. I know we can."

She nodded. "I think you're right. I'd really like to try, because if I lose you now I'll never forgive myself."

His hands traveled down the length of her. Nan heard some warning bells go off in her head but she closed her mind against them and gave herself up to the splendor of his mouth and hands.

He rolled over against her until their full length was touching from head to foot. Nan couldn't remember feeling so tall, so alive in every fiber and nerve ending. He shifted his body until his chest was above her and she was lying prone on the matting. Nan felt the rasp of the hair on his legs as he rubbed them against her smooth skin. The sensation was incredibly exciting.

Slowly, deliberately, he eased the strap of her swimsuit down over her shoulder exposing the soft upper curve of her breast. He bent his head over it until she had to grit her teeth to keep from crying out with the ecstasy of his mouth, warm and moist against her skin. She tangled her fingers in the hair at the back of his head and forced his mouth hard against her until they both moaned with pleasure.

The warning bells were gone now. All that was left was a burning need that threatened to overwhelm her. His hips had begun to move in a slow rhythm as old as the world itself. All that separated them was the thin fabric of their swimsuits, and even that could not temper the heat which generated between them. She ached for him.

Robert's hand drifted downward to the curve of her hip until he cupped it in his hand. "Let's go in to the bunk. I want to make love to you."

Her eyes beseeched him not to move. "I can't wait that long."

"Oh God, Nan." He groaned.

She shook her head. "Kiss me."

His mouth came down over hers in a heat of passion too powerful to control. Slowly, as if in a trance, Nan reached for the other strap to her suit and slid it down over her shoulder.

Chapter Fifteen

ROBERT HAD OBVIOUSLY, until now, tried hard to keep himself under control but they had passed the point of no return. The flame that ignited their blood threatened to engulf them. He pulled at her suit in an effort to slide it down but the zipper held it in place. Nan rolled to one side to release it, but at that moment there was a horrifying crash.

Robert jerked to a sitting position. "My God, what was that?"

Nan, her senses slowly returning, covered herself and sat up, nodding toward the mast of a sailboat protruding over the top of the cabin. "I think we were rammed by one of the boats."

Robert got up awkwardly, then reached for a towel and tied it around his middle, over his trunks as he half ran toward the bow of the boat. Grabbing hold of the rail, he looked down into the water. "Are you all right?" he yelled.

"I guess so. Man, where'd you come from? We sure didn't see you."

Robert's face was red with suppressed anger. "I've anchored here for the last hour. Why don't you watch where you're going?"

"Now he tells us." The boy laughed. "Hey man, can you help us right the boat? I think my arm's busted."

Robert threw the towel on the deck and made a clean dive into the water. A few minutes later they had the sailboat righted, and a sleek power boat had pulled alongside to offer assistance. It didn't take long to assess the damage. The cruiser was barely scratched but the sailboat had a sizable ding in its Fiberglas hull. It was just a question of time until it started taking on water. The boy's arm was broken, there was no doubt about that.

Robert was quick to take charge of the situation. He asked the power boat driver to take the injured boy to the hospital while he helped the other boy into the cruiser. After considerable discussion they all agreed that the sailboat would stay afloat until they were able to tow it into the marina. Once the tow line was secured, Robert hauled in the anchor on the cruiser and moved the throttle slowly forward until the sailboat followed like an obedient puppy on a leash. A few yards away, the captain of the power boat signaled that everything looked shipshape, then moved the throttle forward to the full and rose to a plane on the crest of the water.

The boy looked forlorn as his friend sped away toward the hospital in the other boat. "Jeez. My dad is gonna kill me. I wish I'da broken my arm. Maybe he'd go a little easier on me. Ya know?"

Robert nodded. "It's a hard life any way you look at it."

Nan came to stand beside him at the wheel. As she looked up at him, he looked down at her and their eyes telegraphed a message. All of a sudden they both burst into laughter and it was several seconds later before they could stop. Robert knotted his fingers in her hair and pulled her into the curve of his arm. "I'm sorry, Nan. We'll make up for it later."

She put her arm around his waist and rested her head against his chest. "I'm counting on it."

It seemed like hours before they were free to go. Even though Robert was in no way to blame for the accident, there were countless reports to be filled out in triplicate. Nan was sorry for the boy, even though she knew he deserved whatever he got. The authorities were less than sympathetic, but Robert finally convinced them that he should be allowed to take the boy home to talk to his father before any charges were made.

He had offered to take Nan home first but she could tell it was a token gesture. She was glad. It was early and she enjoyed being with Robert, even under these circumstances. It was close to three hours later when they were again alone. Robert got into the car after seeing the boy's father and exchanging insurance information. He looked at his watch. "We never did get around to eating. Do you want to go back to the boat?"

"I . . . I don't know. Maybe we could just stop for a hamburger or something. It seems a little anticlimactic to go back to the boat."

"Right. There's a hamburger place just down the street."

Later, when they were sitting in a booth in a far corner, he reached for her hand. "I know it's customary for the guy to give the girl her ring when he asks her to marry him but I wanted to wait and buy something that I knew you'd like. Besides, I was afraid that buying the ring ahead of time was like asking for bad luck." He grinned.

She looked at him in disbelief. "Don't tell me you're superstitious."

"No . . . not really. Just careful."

"Robert Easton, you are a man of contradictions. I didn't think they made men more businesslike, or more practical than you, and now I find you believe in luck."

The corners of his mustache twitched as it did when he was perturbed. "I make my own luck, but I wasn't about to take a chance on losing you."

She laced her fingers in his. "Your chances of losing me are so remote as to be inconceivable."

"Promise?"

"Promise. What could possibly come between us now?"

"Lance."

"No, Robert. Not unless you let him. If I have any feeling for him it's pity, but I have no intention of letting him ruin my life. You, on the other hand, may have a half-dozen slinky blondes tucked away for safekeeping."

"Not even a brunette. I was completely fancy-free until you

came into my life, and I'd intended to stay that way."

"Sorry?"

"The only thing I'm sorry about is that we were interrupted this afternoon."

She lowered her gaze and drew a pattern with her finger in the ring of water made by her iced tea glass. "But think of what we have to look forward to."

"I'm thinking, I'm thinking. You haven't told me how soon we can set the date."

"Would a month from now be all right?"

"So long?"

She smiled. "I was hoping you'd say that. How about three weeks?"

"Make it two and you've got a deal."

"Then how about the fourteenth?"

"It sounds good to me."

She grinned. "I think I'll handle the business affairs once we're married. I was willing to settle for the tenth."

He shook his head. "One of these days, lady, you're going to push me too far."

"Promises, promises."

He reached for a lock of her hair and curled it around his finger. "Let's go up to my place."

"Now? Oh, I don't know. Maybe it's not such a good idea."

"There's something I want to show you."

"It's not that I don't trust you, Robert. I know it's silly to cling to moral codes which seem outdated, but this afternoon I really went out of control. I know in my heart that it wouldn't have changed anything, but I want so much for us to get off to a good start. Can you understand how I feel?"

He nodded. "I told you once before that we wouldn't do anything you didn't want to."

She smiled wryly. "You're a big help. I know I could never convince you I'm an unwilling partner. I wouldn't even be able to convince myself."

He moved closer and she could feel the muscles ripple in his thigh. "It would take some doing, that's for sure. Look, Nan. If it means that much to you, two weeks isn't that long to wait. I'll keep the shower set on ice water."

"Mine?"

He grinned. "No. You're strictly on your own. Come on. Just a quick stop at my apartment, then I'll take you home."

The King Midas was crowded with groups of people coming and going to the various casinos and night clubs on the strip. The crowds changed with the seasons. Summer brought the older, wealthier tourist who was bent on making the rounds of the clubs. It also brought the convention crowds. Winter brought, along with the ever-present gamblers, the ski crowd, the outdoor enthusiasts of the younger generation. Robert threaded the car through the jammed parking garage to his own private stall. Then they walked up to the second floor and took a private express elevator which by-passed the hotel rooms and led to the penthouse suite on one of the upper floors. A maid greeted Robert and asked if she could be of service but he shook his head and thanked her as she got off the elevator on the floor below theirs.

Nan looked around her with approval. The elevator had opened onto a foyer decorated with an Oriental theme. Pastel silk wallpaper depicted a Japanese garden overlooking the Sea of Japan with its giant boulders and crooked pines washed with sea spray. Pale green velvet carpeting matched silk drapes which covered a large window. There was only one door; a carved double door of ivory enamel trimmed with gold leaf. He fished his keys from his pocket, unlocked it, and ushered her in as he pressed a button on the wall, flooding the room with subdued light.

Nan caught her breath. "Why, it's lovely. I had no idea it would be so large."

"I sometimes use it to entertain business associates, so it has to be roomy. Can I get you something to drink? A glass of wine, a cocktail?"

"Maybe a very small glass of white wine."

He pushed a button on a control panel in the wall and a drapery separated leaving what looked like a paneled wall. He pushed another button and the wall turned to reveal a compact, completely equipped bar. Taking goblets from a glass cabinet, he poured two glasses of wine and offered one to her.

"To you, Nan. For saying yes when I asked you to marry me." They clinked glasses.

"And to you, Robert, for asking me. I'll try hard to make you happy."

He bent down and kissed her forehead. "I have the feeling you won't have to try very hard. Just being with you makes me happier than I've ever been in my life." He put his glass down and reached for her. His arms were warm and inviting. Nan felt the heat flow through her body and she knew it wasn't because of the wine. She ran a quick tongue across her lips.

"Hey. Are you going to show me the rest of your apartment? I don't want you to get sidetracked."

"You saw right through me, didn't you? First I ply you with liquor and then..."

"And then look out because I happen to be wise to your ways. Is this the kitchen through here?"

"Yep. It's small, but there's a dining area, powder room, bath, two bedrooms separated by a dressing room, and of course the den." When they were back in the living room Robert walked over to the outside wall. "You haven't seen the best part." He pushed a button and the twenty-foot wall of drapes separated to reveal a window wall which looked out over the city and Lake Tahoe beyond. In the far distance the mountains were a dense uneven band against the darkening sky. Robert snapped a catch on the glass doors and slid them open.

Nan walked past him onto the narrow balcony and rested her knee against the seat which was built into the railing. "This has to be the best view I've ever seen of the city at night. It's even better than from Heavenly Valley."

"Um. I like it too. But wait till you see the new hotel we're building. It's going to make this place look like peanuts. I'll have to take you to see it. I thought you might want to live in the penthouse when it's finished." He started to tell her more about it when his telephone rang.

Nan wandered back into the living room to look at some of the paintings displayed on his walls. They were original oil paintings and a few matted water colors of California scenes done by local artists. The rest of the room was tastefully decorated in muted pastel colors with shades of blue, green, and turquoise predominating. A bowl of fresh red roses and blue marguerites were centered on the low coffee table. It was plain

to see that Robert was well cared for, even if it was by the
hotel staff. With a little persuasion, she could learn to be very
comfortable here. And with Robert to come home to . . . the
thought left her breathless.

He came back from the den a moment later. "Sorry. It was
a business call."

"Something you have to attend to tonight?"

He looked apologetic. "I should. It's important. I told Mr.
Farmdale I'd meet him in the lobby in a few minutes. It won't
take more than forty-five minutes." He stroked his mustache.
"I could have Arthur take you home but I'd much rather you'd
wait."

"I'll wait. Take your time, Robert. I'll be just fine."

"Are you sure you don't mind? I'm not ready to say goodnight."

"Neither am I."

He reached into his pocket. "Great. But before I go downstairs I want you to have this. It's a poor substitute for an
engagement ring but we'll go together and pick that out tomorrow night. Come closer."

She bent down and he fastened a necklace behind her head.
It was a gold, serpentine chain with the gold globe and eagle,
the emblem of the Easton empire.

He kissed her warmly, and with barely controlled passion.
"There." He smiled. "That makes it official. From now on you
belong to me."

She reached up and put her hands on each side of his face.
"And you to me, Robert Easton."

He grinned. "You said you'd make me pay one day, but
there's no doubt in my mind that I'm getting the best of the
deal."

"Don't be too sure, Robert. You don't know what I'm thinking at this very moment."

He looked surprised. "I wish I had time to go into that, but
Mr. Farmdale is waiting. God, I hate to leave you like this,
Nan. Make yourself comfortable and I'll be back as soon as
I can."

After he closed the door to the apartment Nan floated out
onto the balcony on her own special cloud.

A slight breeze coming in off the lake lifted the hair from

the back of her neck. She shaded her eyes against the glare of the lights below until she could see the faint smudge of the island at Emerald Bay. The few sailboats which remained on the water were headed in toward the marina as if reluctant to admit the splendid day had drawn to a close.

And it *had* been a lovely day. Nan felt her stomach flip as she remembered the rasp of Robert's mustache against her breast. God, it had been a long time since she had known the pleasure of a man. . . . She needed the special warmth that only a man could give her. Her body ached for it.

Robert had been gone just a few minutes. Maybe a shower would cool her down. Unbuttoning her blouse as she went, Nan hurried down the hallway to the elegantly appointed bathroom.

She turned the shower on full after having wrapped a towel around her hair. The bathroom had everything: thick white carpeting, huge fluffy towels in turquoise and white, and marvelous little bars of scented soap, but there wasn't a shower cap in sight. She let the water sting her skin, driving away the relentless craving. But the effect was momentary. As she stepped from the shower she saw the flash of her body in the mirror. It was a good body, long and supple, and smooth; made to please a man. She felt the heat rise in her face. That particular thought had never occurred to her before but suddenly she wanted very much to please . . . and be pleased.

She picked up her watch from the marble vanity. Fewer than fifteen minutes had gone by. She had plenty of time to dress. Wrapping herself sarong fashion in a frosty white towel, she opened the door to Robert's bedroom.

She had seen it in passing when he showed her the rest of the apartment, and she was impressed with the white carpeting, teal blue velvet chairs, and the matching bedspread. But seeing it alone, Nan was overcome by the subtle reminders of his masculinity. Brushing her bare feet across the carpet, she started to enter the room when she became aware of his presence.

She turned quickly. "Oh! I'm sorry. I didn't expect you so soon."

"Don't apologize. The pleasure is all mine. Mr. Farmdale was more cooperative than I anticipated." She couldn't see his smile but she could hear it in his voice. Nan wasn't sure whether to laugh or cry but Robert made the decision for her.

He came toward her slowly, as if savoring each step. Nan felt totally defenseless as he towered over her in her bare feet, his eyes hot with undeniable hunger. He reached for the towel around her head and parted the fold. It dropped, spilling her hair in a copper cascade around her shoulders as he pulled her against him.

As his mouth covered hers, Nan gave herself over to the sheer joy of his kiss. His voice was husky against her hair when he finally paused to breathe.

"I didn't think it would be possible to want you any more than I did this afternoon. You were so lovely in your little white swimsuit. But seeing you here . . . like this . . . God, how I wish I'd never agreed to your terms."

Nan felt a surge of power as pagan as the act itself and she was delirious with the joy of it. She brushed her mouth across his chest where his shirt opened to a deep V. He shuddered.

"Don't do this to me, Nan."

"Be still and take your punishment," she whispered. "I told you I'd make you pay one day."

He held her off at arm's length and searched her face.

"Do I have anything to say about this?"

"Not a thing. Does that fact bother you?"

"Not at the moment." He grinned crookedly. "Where do we go from here?"

"All in good time, my friend. You were the one who liked to take things slow and easy." Her fingers slid down his shirtfront as she unbuttoned it, then pulled it free of his pants. Slipping her hands underneath, she wrapped her arms around his bare back and leaned against his chest.

"Nan. *Nan!*" His voice was tightly controlled. "I don't know what you have in mind but you can only tempt me so far."

"And then what?" She laughed.

"And then I make the rules."

"Is that a promise?"

"I'd call it that."

"Um. Just how far do I have to tempt you?"

"About that far, I'd say."

She smiled up at him. "You mean like this?" Putting her

mouth against his bare chest she traced a line of fire with her tongue, from one side to the other.

He drew his breath in a deep gasp then bent down and picked her up. In a moment they were on the bed and he was beside her as his hands tore at the towel which was knotted at her breast. She lifted herself to help him. In another moment, his own clothing lay in a heap on the floor and he stood over her. Her pulse quickened as she looked up at him with a yearning too intense to hide.

"Make love to me Robert. Now."

Chapter Sixteen

WHEN IT WAS over they lay exhausted in each other's arms. For the first time in her life Nan felt complete...and completely happy.

Robert turned to look at her then lifted himself until he was resting on one elbow as he gazed down at her. He bent to kiss her breast where the force of their lovemaking had left an imprint of the Easton medallion which she still wore around her neck.

"I left my brand on you. Does it hurt?"

She shook her head. "It would hurt much more if you had refused."

"No chance of that. We went beyond that when I walked into the room and saw you standing there."

"Like a shameless wanton?"

"Like the woman I love," he said as he pulled her under him and took her again.

Nan decided, on the way up to the lodge the next morning, not to let anyone know that she was engaged until Robert had given her the ring. Much as she hated to admit it, she had her own streak of superstition and she wasn't about to push her luck, not when everything was nearly too perfect to be real.

The limousine which brought Craig was much later than usual—not surprising, since Laura was with him. From the glow on their faces it was apparent that they had been seeing a great deal of each other.

Laura came over to Nan and reached for her hands. "I know I should be at work but Craig was very persuasive. Besides, I wanted to talk to you." She led Nan over to a corner where it was comparatively quiet. "I know you'll never believe this, but Craig has asked me to marry him."

Nan grabbed her and hugged her tightly. "Oh, Laura, I am so happy for you. After all these years. . . . You must be terribly excited."

Laura nodded. "Yes, but more than that, I'm just plain scared."

Nan sat down and pulled Laura into a chair facing her. "Scared? I don't understand. Isn't this what you've been wanting?"

She nodded slowly. "Ten years ago I would have given an arm to have him propose to me, but I was younger then, and less vulnerable. God, Nan, it's taken me years to build up to where I am now. I don't know if I have the courage to sell out and chase after him. What if he decides in six months that he's tired of me and wants out? I couldn't start all over. Not at my age."

Nan reached for her hand. "It's a big decision, Laura, but it's one you'll have to make for yourself. No one else can tell you what to do."

"You're a big help."

"I guess you have two alternatives. You can marry him and start a new life . . ."

Laura nodded. "Or I could turn him down and go on as I was before this all happened."

"But could you do that? Could you really put him out of your mind as if you hadn't been reunited?"

Laura gazed steadily at her for a few moments, then shook her head. "I guess that's it, isn't it? I've always been in love with Craig, and I always will be." She grinned. "Well, they

say there's a fortune to be made in real estate down in L.A.
What the hell.... You can't stop the world. I guess I'll take
a crack at being Mrs. Craig Martindale. I have a sneaking
hunch he'll keep me so busy I won't even have time to apply
for a broker's license."

"I wish you all the best in the world, Laura. I'll miss you
more than you'll ever know."

"Listen, kid. It breaks my heart that things aren't settled for
you. I'm going to worry about you and that ex-husband of
yours. He scares me sometimes."

"I wasn't going to tell anyone quite yet, but Robert has
asked me to marry him."

Laura let out a whoop. "Fan-tas-tic! I can't believe it happened so fast. Oh... that's right, you did say you had known
him before. Oh, Nan, I'm so thrilled for you. Have you set the
date?"

"The fourteenth. Neither of us wanted to wait. We're just
going to have a small wedding."

"You've got to invite me."

Nan reached over and hugged her. "I will, Laura. You're
like family."

They talked over their plans until the cast appeared on the
set, then Laura scurried off toward the waiting limousine to
return to her office.

Robert called Nan just before quitting time and told her he'd
be waiting for her when she got home. He was and Nan felt
a surge of happiness as he opened the door of the car and held
out his arms to her. *Here,* she thought, *is everything I've ever
dreamed about since I stopped being a child. For the first time
in my life I know what it's like to be fully and completely happy.*

He put his arm around her as they walked into the house.
"I got a call from the builder today. They're putting the final
touches on the new hotel and I want you to have a look at it
before they turn the decorators loose. If you decide you want
to live there I'd like you to make the decisions as to color and
what kind of furniture you'll want in the penthouse."

"But I don't know anything about decorating a place like
that." She spread her hands wide. "This is the extent of my
decorating ability, and most of it was chosen by my mother."

"I can't see a thing wrong with it, but the choice is up to you." He sank down into a soft chair. "For that matter, I wonder if you would rather continue to live here. It's plain to see you have a strong emotional attachment for your parents' home."

Nan folded her arms across her chest. "It's true, I'll miss this house, but it's foolish to hold onto the past. Besides, it's so far from your office. If we live closer by, maybe you'll be able to spend more time with me."

He reached for her hand and pulled her down onto his lap. "I like the way you think." He nuzzled the back of her neck. "I like the way you smell. In fact I like everything about you."

She giggled. "That tickles."

"It's supposed to." He spread the fingers of her left hand onto his knee. "I found a ring I think you might like. After we stop at the new hotel, I want you to see it."

She pulled herself away. "In that case, give me a few minutes to change and I'll be right with you."

She took a lightning-quick shower and slipped into a pale green crepe de Chine shirtwaist dress with an ivory and green sleeveless jacket. A pair of ivory high-heeled sandals and a matching ivory clutch purse completed the outfit which she topped off with a long, knotted double strand of marbled green jade beads.

He was out on the deck when she found him. He turned and looked her over approvingly. "I wish my dad could have seen you. He always said that if I could marry a girl with brains and a sense of independence, I'd be lucky. But if I could find one who was also beautiful, I'd have more than my share of blessings."

She walked into his arms and when he kissed her Nan knew beyond a shadow of a doubt that he loved her, not just for the thrill of a moment's passion, but with a love to build on for a lifetime.

She stood beside him as they looked out over the lake. "I wish they could have been here to share with us . . . your parents and mine. I want so much for them to have known you."

"We have each other. I guess that's all we can ask." He nestled his face in her hair. "Come on. Let's go look at our new hotel."

When they were in the car Nan looked up at him. "I didn't even ask you the name of it. Is it on the Nevada side?"

He glanced at her quizzically. "I thought you knew . . . being in the real estate business."

She looked at him dryly. "I'm not into buying and selling hotels as yet. I'm strictly homes and condominiums. What's it called?"

"It's over on the east shore. We called it Tiffany Towers."

Nan felt the color drain from her face. Reaching for the shoulder harness she tore it off as if it were the sudden cause of her inability to breathe. She had to have heard wrong. He couldn't possibly have said Tiffany Towers.

Robert looked at her with alarm. "My God, Nan. What's wrong? Are you ill? You look like you've seen a ghost."

"I . . ." She cleared her throat with an effort. "What did you say the name of your hotel is?" She prayed that she had heard wrong, but she had heard correctly.

His voice was puzzled. "It's the Tiffany Towers."

"But that hotel belongs to the Amherst Corporation."

"Sure. It's one of our companies. It belongs to Easton Enterprises."

"Stop the car. I want to get out!"

He looked at her in disbelief. "Are you crazy?"

She grabbed at the wheel and he had to fight her off to keep from careening into cars parked along the curb. "Damn it, Nan. What the devil are you trying to do? Get us killed?"

"Just pull over."

His lips were white and the rest of his face had taken on a deep red color. "I don't know what this is all about but if this is your idea of a joke you'd better forget it."

He spotted a parking place and eased the car into it with shaking hands. "All right. Let's have it."

Tears welled up in her eyes. "You bastard. You filthy greedy bastard. How could you have pretended to love me when you killed my mother?"

He brushed a hand across his eyes. "My God, I must be having a nightmare. What on earth are you talking about?"

"Amherst Corporation. As if you didn't know. They, *you*, that is, took over the nursing home where my mother was staying and made all the patients move to another building. Do you know how many patients died after that? Three! Three people died just so that you could build your bloody hotel."

"Oh come on, Nan. You can't blame me for that. Those patients were moved to cleaner, brighter rooms in a new facility. We did everything we could to make sure they were comfortable."

As Nan listened to his words, all the bitterness, all the pain surrounding her mother's death flooded back into her thoughts. As if it had happened yesterday, she could hear her mother pleading, begging not to be moved. She began sobbing with all the agony of tears too long held back. Robert just sat there, staring out of the window.

"It was a long time ago, Nan. If it hadn't been my company it would have been another. Lakehaven was an old, old building. It was falling apart. Years ago when it was built it was an ideal location, but now with all the traffic and noise, it was no place for a convalescent home. We traded them the property on Woodland Drive and paid nearly a third of the cost on the new facility. We bent over backward to help them. It cost us a small fortune."

"Money! That's all you really care about, isn't it?"

"Be fair. If there had been any other way I'd have taken it. You of all people have to know how hard it is to find property around the lake where it's still possible to build a hotel."

"Fair! You don't know the meaning of the word. How fair is it to force someone out of the only home they'll ever know? Turn the car around. I want to go home."

He looked at her for a moment then slowly eased the car out of the space and made a U-turn at the next corner. "Let's go for a drive. I think we need to talk about this."

"Talk? There's nothing left to say. As long as I live I'll be haunted by my mother's face the day they moved her to the new home. Can you talk that away? Or maybe you'd like to buy your way out of it like you did the owners of the nursing home."

"That's not only ridiculous, it's inaccurate. What did you expect us to do? Just sit around and wait until all the people who wanted to remain in the nursing home died off? It would have been hell for them. There was building going on all around the old place—Jackhammers, trucks, cement mixers. You can't tell me the patients could have found any degree of comfort if they had remained there. The only ones who wanted to stay were those who were too far gone to benefit from decent surroundings."

"I don't want to talk about it. Just take me home."

"I thought we were going to look for a ring."

Nan drew a deep breath. "A ring! Do you think I could marry you, knowing what I know now?"

His mouth drew into a tight line as if he were having trouble controlling it. "Please don't say that. You're upset. God, if I'd known I would have explained it all to you instead of letting you find out like this. Don't do anything you'll be sorry for, Nan. I love you. I want to marry you. Give me a chance to make it all up to you."

"Sure. Right after you make it up to my mother."

They rode in silence the rest of the way to Nan's house. She jumped out of the car before it had even stopped, then ran to the house, unlocked the door and slammed it behind her. She thought she heard Robert calling her name for some time after that, but she lay on the bed and covered her head with a pillow. Darkness had fallen when she finally got up. Robert was gone.

It was like walking through a nightmare. The creature who looked back from the mirror bore little resemblance to Nan. Her face was ravaged by tears, her eyes red and puffy, her skin devoid of color. She ran her hand through her hair. It felt as if it had never been combed. Pulling off her dress, she threw it on the floor and crawled into bed.

The telephone rang. She ignored it as long as possible, then took it off the hook and shoved it under a comforter. About three in the morning she woke again and found it impossible to get to sleep. Going into the den she collapsed into a chair and sat there staring at the wall until daylight.

For a while Nan toyed with the idea of not going to work. She was a mess. It would take more than makeup to cover the damage done to her face, but habit won out. She would have to face the world eventually. After a quick shower she put on a pants suit and tied a scarf over her head. Late or not, she was going to stop by the cemetery on her way to work. Though she had been there just a few days before, she felt the need to go again.

The gate was still locked but she managed to scramble over the low wall surrounding the small cemetery and make her way toward the family plot. She had forgotten flowers. Too bad. The roses in the garden were beautiful. Her mother had always loved roses. Nan stood by the headstone and traced the fine grooves in the marble wreath.

You were right after all, Mother, she thought. *I ended up getting hurt, just as you said I would. I never should have accepted that first date with him.* "I'm sorry, Mother. I'm sorry," she whispered.

Being there for those few minutes seemed to help. She managed to pull herself together enough to go to work. When she got there a half dozen different people told her there were messages waiting for her in the trailer. No doubt they were from Robert. She ignored them. It was over. Better not to drag it out.

Craig came up to her a short time before call. "Lord, you look like death warmed over. I'm sorry about Lance. I wish there was something I could do. Do you want the day off?"

"Lance? What're you talking about?"

He looked embarrassed. "I thought you knew. He was in a brawl last night at the King Midas. I guess he broke up some of the tables because they refused to let him gamble. They threw him out. I'm surprised they didn't throw him in jail but I guess he had Robert to thank for that."

"What do you mean? What did Robert have to do with it?"

He shrugged. "Well, I just heard that your Mr. Easton offered to take care of the damages as long as Lance left the premises."

Nan felt numb. Lord, what next? She repressed the urge to start running as fast as she could and not stop until she was free, free, free, of all her problems. But running wouldn't do it. She had learned that a long time ago. She breathed a sigh of relief when the call was sounded and the cast began filing in for the first take. She needed something to occupy her mind.

They were just breaking for lunch when Laura drove into the lot. Craig hurried over to her and started to kiss her but she held him off as she spoke to him. He nodded then linked his arm in hers until they separated by the lunch trailer. Laura came over toward Nan and put her arm around her. "Let's take a walk."

Nan felt the tears burn her eyelids. "You know, don't you?"

"Yes. Robert called me this morning. He's been trying to reach you for hours. It's a dumb thing you're doing, Nan."

"You can't possibly know, Laura, so please don't say anything."

"Like hell. If you think I'm going to let you ruin your life without even trying to stop you, you're crazy. I didn't know your mother but I know this. She's dead and you're alive. Let her rest in peace, for God's sake, and get on with the business of living. If you don't, you're going to be lonely an awfully long time. And *that* is something I know plenty about."

Nan turned away from her. "I appreciate what you're trying to do, Laura, but you weren't with my mother when she died. I was. If they hadn't moved her to another home, she'd still be alive."

"Bull. You don't know that. You just want to believe it. You're feeling guilty because she's dead and you're not. If you stop and think about it I'll bet she laid the guilt trip on you plenty of times when she was still alive."

Nan's eyes blazed. "Stop it, Laura. You're going too far. I'd hate to lose the best friend I've ever had."

Laura put her arms around her. "I'm sorry, Nan. I'd die rather than see you get hurt. But it's killing me what you're doing to yourself...and to Robert. He deserves better from you."

Nan started to say something, but Laura raised her hand. "Okay. I've said my piece. From now on it's up to your own good sense. Just one thing more. Robert said he'd be waiting for you. He's hurting, Nan. Really hurting."

She turned and went back to her car without even saying goodbye to Craig.

Craig came over after a while and would have tried to comfort her but Nan brushed him aside. The rest of the day she drove herself to the point of exhaustion. There was really nothing for her to do but she found work, even if it were only dusting the furniture and pulling the few weeds in the flower beds.

She worried about Laura for the rest of the day. When Nan got home from work she tried to call her and mend their fences but Laura's Record-a-call was on and Nan hung up without leaving a message. A few minutes after she hung up, her own phone rang and Nan assumed it was Laura. It was Robert.

"Wait, Nan. Don't hang up. I've got to talk to you." There was a pause. She didn't want to talk to him but the sound of his voice was so dear. . . . How could she love him so and hate him so much at the same time?

There was an unfamiliar hoarseness to his words. "Don't do this to me, Nan. I love you more than anything in the world, and I know you love me. I'd do everything possible to change things in the past, but there's nothing I can do. Don't you understand that?"

She caught her lower lip between her teeth to keep from crying and slowly replaced the phone on the hook. It rang again within seconds and she lifted the receiver, then shoved the phone under the bed with her foot.

The lake was like velvet when she took out the rowboat. She had hoped for waves, large waves that would make her concentrate all her energy on keeping the boat afloat, but it was like a millpond, clear and crystalline, chased with emerald shadows among the patches of azure sky reflected in its depths. In the distance a sailboat, becalmed and still, waited for an errant breeze. It looked familiar. Was it the boat they had towed into shore last night? No. They couldn't have repaired it so soon. She hunched forward resting the oars, and let her gaze slide from one thing to the next, aimlessly, without direction. Like her life, she thought. Was this the way it would be from now on? Laura had said that you couldn't stop the world but Nan decided she had, at least her own world.

Her gaze fell on a dried flower that Robert had picked the night they had taken the boat out. Apparently it had fallen from her hair. How long would she find remnants of him decorating her life? She squeezed her eyes tight. There had to be some way to stop thinking of him. Even during her divorce from

Lance she had never felt such agony and desolation. One thing for sure, she'd never find the answer in the boat. Lake Tahoe, Emerald Bay, Robert's boat, they all held too many memories for her. She lifted the oars and pointed the bow in the direction of her pier.

Somehow Nan managed to get through the evening. She took out the family album and devoured the snapshots of her mother and father. It helped reaffirm the sense of rightness in her decision. The only bad moment came when she saw the photo of her pet dog who had died at age twelve. Her father had comforted her by saying that the time came when one had to let go. She blinked her eyes. To let go was like thinking they never existed. She couldn't let it happen. She would never forget her parents.

Someone came to her door twice during the evening but she didn't answer. Nor did she look to see who it was. If it was Robert she didn't know if she was strong enough to keep from running after him.

Just before going to bed she put the phone back on the hook. It rang almost immediately. Nan picked it up. "Hello."

"Hello, Miss Gilliam. This is Mr. Easton's service. He has been trying desperately to get in touch with you. He wanted me to tell you he would. . ." Nan hung up. It was better not to know. She left the receiver on the floor.

She woke the next morning with the taste of stale sponges in her mouth, and it occurred to her she hadn't eaten anything since noon the day before. She forced a piece of dry toast down with a cup of tea.

When she arrived at the lodge Craig took one look at her and grabbed her by the arm as he steered her toward the trailer. "What you need is a shot of brandy. If that stays down we'll feed you a bowl of soup."

"Please, Craig. Just the thought is enough to make me heave."

"Don't argue. I know what I'm doing."

Apparently he did. The brandy spread through her body like molten lava. She even managed to swallow a few sips of chicken soup before she pushed it away.

"Ugh. That's enough. I'm dying of a broken heart, not the flu." She managed a smile.

He grinned. "Good. Broken hearts we can mend. The flu..." He waggled his hand. "I've got some news for you. Laura and I got married last night. I owe it all to you."

Nan reached up and took his face in her hands. "I'm so awfully glad. Be good to her, Craig. Laura's easily hurt, for all her tough exterior."

"Don't worry. I'd give my life for that stubborn broad. I never did stop loving her, but you knew that all along."

Nan nodded. "At least I thought so...but I'm really glad to hear you say it. Will you take a honeymoon?"

"As soon as she can find someone to take over the realty office and after we finish shooting. The show must go on, you know." He grinned, but Nan knew that he really meant it.

"Speaking of the show, you were supposed to start shooting a half-hour ago. Don't let the schedule slip because of me. I'm fine now. Thanks, Craig."

"You're sure?"

She nodded. "I think I'll get a cup of coffee and then I'll be right out."

He gave her arm a quick squeeze and got up from the stool. "Later."

The short-order cook who ran the mess trailer asked her if she wanted anything else before he left. They were shooting the hot-tub scene this morning and some of the crew had found a place where they could look without being seen on the set. He pushed the radio across the counter and moved the coffee pot within easy reach then hurried out.

Nan sipped the thick black liquid and made a face. She should have stayed with the soup. Even the music was disappointing. The only music she could find as she turned the dial was sad and lonely country and Western, or blues more appropriate to a night-club setting. She had just reached up to turn it off when the announcer broke into the song.

"We interrupt this program to bring you a news bulletin. A report is just in that an unidentified sniper, located on the roof of the King Midas Hotel, is firing random shots at pedestrians along the strip. The police have cordoned off the area immediately surrounding the hotel and the adjoining annex. As yet no one has been seriously injured but citizens are urged to avoid this area since as yet it has not been determined how many people are involved in the shoot-out. So far, one and possibly two people have been spotted on the roof. This station is sending an on-the-spot reporter to cover the scene and will bring you further news as soon as it becomes available."

Nan felt her palms begin to sweat. Had Robert gone to work today? Surely they would evacuate the buildings before they did anything else. He had to be safe. He *had* to.

Chapter Seventeen

A MINUTE LATER the announcer came back on the air. "An update on the sniper situation atop the King Midas Hotel. Police are evacuating the buildings within shooting range of the sniper. No word yet as to his identity. He appears to be a white male in his early thirties, dark hair, wearing a business suit. One source says that it appeared the man was possibly deranged or had been drinking heavily. We'll have more news as it becomes available."

A half-hour later Nan was still listening to the radio when the station came on with its live report from the scene. The noise from spectators nearly drowned out the voice of the announcer but she was able to catch most of it.

He sounded excited and a little breathless. "It appears now that there are in fact two men on the roof of the King Midas Hotel here at Stateline. But talk now is that the second man is a hostage rather than another sniper as was previously reported. As yet authorities have no clue as to the motive behind

173

the hostage situation but are attempting at this moment to set up a communication system between the sniper and their riot control unit."

The reporter spent the next ten minutes interviewing people who were watching the stand-off as eagerly as if they were watching a team of high rollers. The reporter said that vacationers had begun to stream out of the casinos in droves, leading at least one official to speculate that the entire episode could be a red herring to cover up a possible robbery attempt at one of the casinos. The call had gone out for all off-duty policemen to report to work.

Nan was joined at the snack bar by some of the crew who were on their first break. Conversation was limited as they listened eagerly to each news flash. It had been going on for over two hours when the announcer came on live from the scene.

"Word has just come down that the sniper has been positively identified. We repeat. The sniper holding the hostage atop the King Midas Hotel has been identified as Lance Hendricks, formerly employed as an emcee in the Golden Slipper Club at the King Midas Hotel. Hendricks was recently fired from the position which he held for several years and it is rumored that his dismissal was a possible motive for the present sniper-hostage situation. Still no identification of the hostage, a white male, who apparently is being held near the ventilating ducts on the hotel roof."

Nan's hands flew to her face. "Oh, dear God! Lance! Oh God. Oh God!"

One of the crew, apparently realizing what had happened, summoned Craig who hurried out and put his arm around Nan. "What's happening? Is he all right?"

Nan shrugged. "He's gone crazy. That has to be the only explanation. I've got to go to him."

"There's nothing you can do, Nan. This has been building up for a long time. You knew something like this was bound to happen unless he got help."

"But they'll kill him, or he'll hurt somebody before they get him down. I could talk to him."

"All right. If you want to go I'll take you."

She seemed to come out of her trancelike disassociation for

a moment. "No. You're in the middle of shooting. You can't go. I have my car. I'll go alone."

"Like hell." He gave the word to wrap it up for the day and left a call for seven the next morning. "We'll go in the limo. I'll have somebody drop your car off at your place when they go into town."

Once inside the limo, Craig pulled Nan against his shoulder, and she was grateful for the comforting warmth of his arm around her. The station had canceled all its regular programming in favor of the on-the-spot report. They could hear gunfire in the distance and each explosion was like a shot in the heart.

She pressed her knuckles against her teeth. *Dear God, don't let him die this way*, she thought.

The announcer interrupted the loquacious woman he was interviewing. "This urgent message has just been handed to me by the chief of police. They are trying to locate a Mrs. Nan Hendricks otherwise known as Nan Gilliam, a local resident. She is the former wife and next of kin to the sniper. Anyone knowing her whereabouts is urged to contact this station at once." He went on to repeat the announcement but Craig lowered the volume.

"Shall I call in and tell them you're on the way?"

Nan nodded. She couldn't trust her voice to speak.

Craig wasted no time in calling the station on the mobile phone. Immediately he was connected to the command center at the hotel and was speaking with the chief of police. Craig refused to let him speak to Nan but informed the chief they would be there within minutes. Nan was grateful. She needed those few precious minutes to pull herself together.

"It's my fault," she wailed against Craig's shoulder. "I should never have divorced him. He needed me. I knew he did."

"Don't be a fool. You'd blame yourself if the roof fell down on him. You're not that important, Nan. None of us is. People live and die, and sometimes they go crazy in between. The important thing is that we care enough to try to help them. We can't hold ourselves responsible for everything that happens in this world. You did the best you could for Lance. No one could have done more for him."

Words, she thought. *He's just trying to make me feel good.*

Maybe I wanted Lance dead. I don't know. If he dies it's my fault. Almost at the same instant her good sense rejected the thought. Lance was ill. She had tried to help him but he had refused help. Maybe now he'd realize how sick he really was . . . if he lived through it.

As the limousine swung through the barricades and into a cleared area near the patrol cars a row of policemen with night sticks held back the crowd. As Nan emerged from the car, a gunshot split the air and, for an instant, all was silent. Finally someone spoke.

"Hey, I think they got him."

Nan's nails dug into her palms. The policeman took her by the arm and pulled her into a room in an adjoining building. "Here she is, Chief, Miss Gilliam, the sniper's ex."

Craig stayed protectively at Nan's elbow while she was being questioned. A psychiatrist on the scene had been talking to Lance over a megaphone while they were trying to get a walkie-talkie up to him without frightening him into a sudden move. The psychiatrist was concerned by her lack of progress. The only response she had been able to get was a volley of shots.

"We're dealing with a highly disturbed man here," she said to the chief. "There is no way of knowing what he'll do next. We need to sedate him but we can't get close enough to administer the medication."

Nan wrapped her arms around herself. "I've got to go up and talk to him. He'll listen to me."

The psychiatrist shook her head. "Out of the question. He's not hearing what's being said. He's too far out of it. You'd be a sitting duck."

"He won't hurt me."

The psychiatrist shook her head patiently. "You don't understand, my dear. He wouldn't even know you now."

Nan reached for the megaphone. "Let me talk over the horn."

The chief handed it to her. "Just push that button while you talk."

Nan nodded. She held onto it for several minutes before she said anything. Then she looked at Craig with tears in her eyes. "I don't know what to say."

"Of course you do, kid. Just tell him not to be afraid. Tell him you understand how he feels and you want to help him."

Nan nodded. She lifted the megaphone to her mouth and spoke. "Lance, this is Nan." She found she could speak in a normal voice and the sound was still loud in her ears. "I . . . I want to help you, Lance. Please listen to me."

There was no way to know if he heard. They couldn't see him from where they were. Nan had been told that a S.W.A.T. team was trying to get onto the roof from the annex. The chief motioned for her to continue.

"We just want to help you, Lance. What is it you want us to do?" She lifted her finger from the button. "How's he supposed to answer if he doesn't have a horn or a telephone?"

The chief patted her on the arm. "Some of my men are close enough they can hear if he yells. Keep talking to him. If nothing else, it'll distract him."

"So you can go in and kill him. That's it, isn't it?"

"Not at all. We'll do everything we can to bring him down alive, but the safety of the hostage comes first."

"Let me go up there. I need to see him face-to-face."

"I can't do that, ma'am. You wouldn't have a chance."

Craig tightened his grip on her waist. "Don't even think that way, Nan. It would be stupid and you know it."

"But I . . ."

At that moment a policeman in dark-colored fatigues came running up. "We've identified the hostage, Chief. He's Robert Easton. The man who owns this hotel."

Nan felt the ground move out from under her and she fainted dead away.

She was lying on a sofa in the lobby of the hotel when she came to. Craig was sitting at her head and a man in a white uniform was bending over her. He looked satisfied when she opened her eyes.

"There. I told you so, Mr. Martindale. She just went under for a minute. The shock I suppose. She'll be fine now."

"I still think we should get her down to the emergency room."

"The chief said they might need her . . ."

"You know what you can do with the chief."

Nan sat up. "No, please. I don't want to leave. I'm all right. Robert . . . has he been hurt?"

Craig shook his head sympathetically. "We don't know.

From what they can tell, he seems to be all right, but he's tied up."

"What does Lance want? Why is he doing this?"

Craig shrugged. "No one knows for sure. Revenge... frustration? It could be any number of things. He's not rational, they're sure of that."

"If I could just talk to him face-to-face."

"Be reasonable, Nan. What could you actually do?"

She shrugged. "I have to try. I have to."

"They'd never hear of it. If they did, I wouldn't."

"I know." She swung her legs over the edge of the couch. "I'm okay now. Let's go back to the chief. Maybe he knows something else by now." She turned to the ambulance attendant. "Thank you very much. You don't have to worry about me now."

He touched two fingers to his cap, picked up his bag, and walked out.

Craig took her arm as she stood up. She turned toward him and put her hand on his arm. "Wait for me. I'd better go to the ladies room before I go out there. It's just down the hall."

He nodded and she turned and walked quickly away before he could change his mind.

The stairs were just around the curve in the hallway. She took the first flight two at a time. Once on the second floor, Nan detoured down another hall until she came to Robert's private elevator. Luckily, it was deserted. Apparently no one had been told about it. She pushed the button and the door opened immediately. Once inside she searched the selectors and found two that were unmarked. If memory served her right, Robert had pushed the bottom one the night they went to his apartment. That meant the top button must be the roof exit. Without hesitation she jabbed it with her finger and leaned back against the wall as the elevator began its ascent.

She closed her eyes. *Help me, please*, she prayed. The elevator stopped with a jolt. Panic set in at the last minute and she jammed her finger against the CLOSE DOOR button. Now that she was here, what in the name of heaven was she going to do? Cold sweat broke out on her back and ran down between her shoulder blades. She could still turn back. It wasn't too late.

Robert's face flashed before her eyes. "Oh God, I love him so. I need him. If only I hadn't . . ." Her whisper died. It was too late to think about that now. She was here. She had to stop Lance. She was the only one who could do it and keep him alive, keep Robert alive, too.

She slowly took her finger away from the button and the door slid open with a menacing hiss.

"Who's there?" Lance screamed, his voice high and thin. Nan hardly recognized it.

"It's Nan. Don't shoot, Lance. I want to talk to you."

"Go away. I don't want to see you. It's your fault. You let this happen."

"I'm sorry. I just want to help."

"You got me fired. You and him. Fixed the dice so I couldn't win. Broke. Sick. God, I don't want to die."

"You sound sick. You must feel terrible. Let me find a place for you to lie down."

"Can't sleep. They'll get me."

"They have a room ready where you can lie down and sleep for as long as you want. You need that, Lance. You've been working and playing too hard. It's time you had a rest."

He swore loudly. "Can't get any rest. Somebody always at me. Pay this, pay that. Get to work, be funny, make the crowd laugh. It's my turn to laugh, but all I can do is cry."

Nan choked back the tears. "You deserve a rest. Let me take over for a while. I've always helped you. Remember when I took care of you after the glider accident?"

"Regular Florence Nightingale."

She forced a smile. "I used to hate it when you called me that. Let me come over there with you. We'll go down together."

"Always the good little mama, aren't you babes?"

"I don't want you to get hurt. I care about you."

"Do you still love me?"

She hesitated for a long time. "I'm not in love with you, Lance. But I care what happens to you."

He laughed harshly as he stepped out from behind a row of chimneys. "You are so damned honest. If you had lied I wouldn't have trusted you."

Nan had to hold on to the elevator when she saw him. He

looked dreadfully run-down. As he came toward her, the rifle slung under his arm, Nan slowly stepped out onto the roof to meet him. She could see Robert a few yards away, fighting to free his legs from the ropes that bound him.

Lance grinned boyishly. "We're going to get out of this, babes. With you here I know I can beat the system."

"You have to give yourself up, Lance. This is one game you can't win. The odds are against you." She barely heard his response. Over his shoulder she could see that Robert had freed his ankles and was standing up. Slowly he made his way toward them. Nan moistened her lips. She couldn't let Lance know that Robert was free. With his hands bound he was still helpless against the rifle Lance held in his right hand.

At that moment she saw a flash of dark fabric and a shot rang out. At first she thought a chip of concrete had hit her ankle but when she looked blood gushed from the side of her leg and she fell down with a sharp cry. Lance swung around, rifle ready to fire, but as he did, Robert hit him with his crossed hands and Lance slid sideways, his rifle spinning in an arc over the wall.

"You bloody bastards," he yelled. "I should have wasted the lot of you."

Robert held him on the floor and they were soon surrounded by men from the S.W.A.T. team who placed Lance in a straitjacket and cut the ropes which held Robert's wrists.

Robert's gaze never left Nan's face.

She looked at him as if to treasure the memory of his face for the rest of her life.

His voice was husky. "You're hurt. God, I wanted to kill him for that."

"I'm fine, Robert. Just a scratch, that's all."

He bound her ankle tightly with his handkerchief. Then he picked her up. "Hold on. I'm taking you to the hospital."

"No. Wait. I want to ride down with Lance."

Robert looked at her warily. "All right. If that's what you want."

A few minutes later the police chief came over and put his hand on her arm as she lay on the stretcher. "That was a stupid thing to do, but I'm glad it turned out as well as it did."

Nan reached up imploringly. "He's sick. Really sick. Will

they see to it that he gets the help he needs?"

"We'll do the best we can, Mrs. Hendricks...I mean, Miss Gilliam. Mr. Martindale and Mr. Easton have already offered to foot the bills for a lawyer and psychiatrist. Now will you please go along to the hospital?"

Craig came over and brushed her forehead with his lips. "I'd go with you but I have the distinct feeling you won't need me anymore." He glanced up at Robert and grinned. "Keep a tight leash on this one. She's too good to lose."

Robert held her hand all the way to the hospital until they pried him loose in the emergency room. Nan lay on the narrow table, a bit woozy from the pain shot but still aware of the conversation beyond the screen. She recognized the voice of the short, gray-haired woman who was the emergency-room head nurse.

"I'm so pleased to finally have a chance to shake your hand, Mr. Easton. You don't know me but I was at the opening of the new Lakehaven Convalescent Hospital the day you cut the ribbon."

Nan heard Robert mumble something, then the nurse continued. "My mother is a patient there and I just want you to know that if it hadn't been for all the life-support equipment your company donated to the home, she wouldn't be alive today. She nearly died in that old rat-trap they used to call a nursing home."

Nan drew a deep breath. *Is it possible I've been wrong all this time? Have I completely misjudged him and his motives?*

He mumbled his thanks then asked about Nan. The nurse stuck her head around the corner of the screen. "Sure. You can step in here. We're just waiting for them to assign her to a room."

Nan looked up sharply. "A room? I'm not going to stay here. I want to go home."

The nurse came over and checked her pulse. "Don't be silly. You should be admitted overnight. I'm sure the doctor will let you go home tomorrow."

"I thought it was just a flesh wound."

"That's right, but you need to stay off your feet for a while."

Robert put his hand on the nurse's shoulder. "How about if I take her home with me? The staff at the King Midas will be happy to look after her and there is certainly plenty of room."

The nurse blushed under his direct gaze. "Well, of course under those circumstances I don't think the doctor would have any objections."

"Would you find out how soon we can leave, please?"

Nan took a deep breath. It obviously never occurred to the nurse to ask her if she wanted to spend the night at Robert's hotel. Robert had a habit of getting his own way without even trying. He looked at Nan as if waiting for an argument. When none came he bent down and squeezed her hand.

She was installed in a private suite on the floor below his penthouse. A maid helped her settle in and saw to it that she had every comfort available. Oddly enough, Robert disappeared shortly after he had helped her into bed. She was disappointed. They needed desperately to talk things out. There was still considerable restraint between them since Nan had walked out on him, and for all he knew, Nan still felt the same as she had two days ago.

She didn't, of course. Time and her own good sense had taken care of that. She realized that it was time to let go. Her mother was dead. Not because of her move to the new nursing home, and not because of lack of care or caring. She was old. It was her time to die. The doctor had tried to tell Nan that her mother probably didn't even know what she was saying when she begged them not to move her. Maybe it was true, maybe not, but one thing for sure, Robert loved her and she loved him. If he still wanted her she would go to him in an instant.

That is if she knew where he was. He still had not returned. She fell into an uneasy sleep under the watchful eyes of the little Oriental maid.

It was near dark when she woke up. Robert was sitting in the chair by the window. He smiled.

"I love you, Nan."

She fought back the tears that threatened to spill over. "I love you, too. I'm sorry for the things I said..."

He reached over and touched his mouth to her lips. "I don't want to hear any more about that. Do you feel up to a wheelchair ride up to the penthouse?"

She nodded. "I feel fine . . . at last."

"Good. Dinner is waiting for us on the balcony. Are you hungry?"

"A little." She grinned. "Actually, I'm starved."

He pulled a soft dressing gown out of the closet. "This is mine, but I'll roll up the sleeves. Can you get it on?"

She nodded, aware of his clean, masculine scent as he bent over to help her. She wanted him to kiss her but he didn't get the message.

A short time later she was sitting on the balcony with her foot propped up on a silk hassock. Robert came in and sat down near her on the bench which ran along the balcony railing.

"There's one thing I have to know. Have you forgiven me enough to marry me?"

She shook her head but her gaze never left his face. "There's no need to forgive you. It was my fault. I was wrong. If you still want me, yes. I want to marry you more than anything in the world."

His voice trembled. "I was so afraid I'd never hear you say that to me. When?"

"We had talked about the fourteenth."

"That was before I found out you would have agreed to a week. I think it's time we renegotiated. The doctor said you'd be on your feet in two days. How about the tenth?"

A slow smile spread over her face. "Whatever you say."

"It's settled, then." He went over to a cardboard carton which was sitting on one end of the bench. "I've chosen a ring for you. I hope you like it." He picked up a square blue-velvet box and brought it back to where she was sitting. He sat down on the bench, his knee grazing hers, and she felt the familiar surge of heat flow through her.

Then he opened the box, took out a large, square-cut diamond which was surrounded by three perfect emeralds, and slipped it onto her finger. "This means forever, Nan. There's no turning back."

She lifted his hand to her cheek. "I'll never want to as long as I have you. You're everything I want in this whole world."

"Everything? That's hard to believe." He grinned. "As I recall you had some very definite ideas about what you like."

"Oh?" She was puzzled by his change of mood.

He went over to the box and picked up a fresh green head of cabbage. "You said your passions run to raw cabbage." He placed it on her lap. "And cashmere sweaters." He reached into the box and brought out a cloud-soft cardigan of pale blue and put it around her shoulders. "And folded potato chips." He brought out a storage-size plastic bag. "Each one guaranteed to be hand selected from over a hundred bags of potato chips."

Nan started to giggle. "Robert, you are absolutely crazy."

"Oh, but I'm not finished." He picked up a champagne bucket filled with ice. Nestled in the middle was the most enormous dill pickle she had ever seen. He placed it on the table. "The German chocolate cake will be served with dinner, but before then I have something else."

She searched his face.

He looked at her with mock alarm. "Surely you couldn't have forgotten the dandelion fuzz?" He brought out a lucite and silver paperweight in the middle of which was imbedded and preserved forever the seed head of a dandelion. One or two seeds had broken loose and drifted a fraction of an inch from the head, just as if they had been caught by the wind. Nan held it to her cheek.

"How absolutely exquisite. Thank you, Robert . . . for all of my favorite things, but thanks most of all for remembering."

"We've left out the most important thing."

"Oh?"

"Children."

She could feel the blood rush into her face. "You *would* remember that. I felt so embarrassed after I made that remark. You must have thought me frighteningly aggressive."

"I thought you were amazingly honest, and I loved you for it." He picked up her hand and turned the engagement ring on her finger. "I had it made to order. The diamond is the symbol of the strength and vigor of my love for you. The three emeralds are clear and deep like the water of Emerald Bay where I first knew I loved you. But they also symbolize something else. The one thing I couldn't give you tonight."

She lifted an eyebrow. "Children?"

He nodded. "One for each emerald. I thought we'd shoot for three to start."

"Little green children?" She grinned up at him and pulled his face down until their noses touched.

He knotted his fingers in her hair. "Be careful. If it weren't for your ankle we'd start on one tonight."

She brushed her lips across his mustache and sent the blood rushing through her veins. "Promises, promises!"

Introducing a unique new concept in romance novels!
Every woman deserves a...

Second Chance at Love ™

You'll revel in the settings, you'll delight
in the heroines, you may even fall in love with the
magnetic men you meet in the pages of...

SECOND CHANCE AT LOVE

Look for three new
novels of lovers lost and found coming every
month from Jove! Available now:

_____05703-7	FLAMENCO NIGHTS (#1) by Susanna Collins	$1.75
_____05637-5	WINTER LOVE SONG (#2) by Meredith Kingston	$1.75
_____05624-3	THE CHADBOURNE LUCK (#3) by Lucia Curzon	$1.75
_____05777-0	OUT OF A DREAM (#4) by Jennifer Rose	$1.75
_____05878-5	GLITTER GIRL (#5) by Jocelyn Day	$1.75
_____05863-7	AN ARTFUL LADY (#6) by Sabina Clark	$1.75
_____05694-4	EMERALD BAY (#7) by Winter Ames	$1.75
_____05776-2	RAPTURE REGAINED (#8) by Serena Alexander	$1.75
_____05801-7	THE CAUTIOUS HEART (#9) by Philippa Heywood	$1.75

Available at your local bookstore or return this form to:

J JOVE/BOOK MAILING SERVICE
P.O. Box 690, Rockville Center, N. Y. 11570

Please enclose 50¢ for postage and handling for one book, 25¢
each add'l book ($1.25 max.). No cash, CODs or stamps. Total
amount enclosed: $_____ in check or money order.

NAME_____

ADDRESS_____

CITY_____STATE/ZIP_____

Allow three weeks for delivery.   SK-13